Following his brother, Bodb, to a ranch in Texas, Lludd works there as a gargoyle enforcer. He protects not only Bodb, but his mate, their holdings, and make-shift family. Over the last few years, Lludd has watched a number of others find their mates in and around the area. He longs for that himself, but as a gargoyle, he has no safe way to search out that special person who is the other half of his soul. At over a thousand years old, Lludd is losing patience. When Bodb gives him a dressing-down for saying something thoughtless — again — he heads to the barn in a foul mood. Naturally, that's when Lludd stumbles upon his mate, startling him but good — Sheriff Archer Montgomery.

The sheriff had been doing some discreet investigating after receiving an anonymous tip about shady goings-on noticed at the ranch. Introducing Archer to the paranormal world is the easy part. Getting him to accept Lludd is quite a bit harder. Can Lludd find a cure for his foot-in-mouth syndrome before driving Archer away for good?

Courting the Sheriff
Copyright © 2020 Charlie Richards
ISBN: 978-1-4874-3063-4
Cover art by Angela Waters

Published by eXtasy Books Inc or
Devine Destinies, an imprint of eXtasy Books Inc

Look for us online at:
www.eXtasybooks.com or www.devinedestinies.com

COURTING THE SHERIFF
A PARANORMAL'S LOVE BOOK
THIRTY-ONE

BY

CHARLIE RICHARDS

CHAPTER ONE

Stretching slowly, Sheriff Archer Montgomery arched his back. The move caused his morning wood to slide against the sheet. As he relaxed on his mattress, he thought about taking himself in hand.

It has been a while.

Archer reached down and gripped his length. Spreading his legs a little, he flipped off the blanket. While the faint light of dawn filtered through his window, the curtains wide open, he didn't worry about anyone seeing.

Living at the edge of town in a cabin in the woods had its advantages—one of them being privacy.

Groaning softly, Archer began slowly jacking his dick, causing his morning stiffie to thicken to full mast. He stared down at where he played, cupping his balls. With a gentle roll, he stimulated himself.

With the way his cock already oozed a bead of pre-cum, Archer knew it had been way too long since he'd taken time to slip into the larger town over and find a bedmate for a few hours of fun.

Archer hummed as he squeezed the head of his prick, giving himself a pinch of pain. His balls tightened, and he didn't bother trying to stop it. He wanted to get off, and he knew he didn't have a lot of time.

His work as the sheriff kept him way too busy until he managed to hire another couple of deputies.

Thinking of his duties caused Archer's arousal to begin to wane. Growling under his breath, he closed his eyes and

1

brought up the image of his last lay. The man had been bigger than Archer's own six-foot-one. He'd sported deep chocolate skin and broad muscles. The stranger had easily man-handled him in bed, holding him down and pounding into his body.

Recalling the sensation, Archer groaned. He released his balls and pressed a finger into his hole. The dry stretch burned deliciously as he began fingering himself. At the same time, Archer sped up the speed of his jacking.

Archer shuddered as he brushed his prostate. His balls pulled tight. He grunted as his orgasm crested, washing his senses in blissful tingles. Humming roughly, he slowed his hand and relaxed, letting his body float on the light after-shocks.

As Archer slowly came to his senses, he released his prick and pulled his finger free of his chute. His ass clenched spastically a couple of times, and he already missed the sensation of being filled.

"Ugh. I need to get laid."

Swiping his fingertips through a glob of his semen, Archer brought it to his lips. He licked it from his fingers. His slightly salty flavor burst across his tongue.

There was something about eating a man's seed that he just loved.

Archer had never discussed his obsession with the masculine flavor with anyone. He'd never had a regular lover he'd been that comfortable with, and due to his heavy work schedule, lovers had been few and far between. With hook-ups, he always used protection, even for blowjobs, so he rarely had the opportunity to taste other men.

Once Archer cleaned himself, he flopped his arms to his side and licked his lips. He swallowed a couple of times as he thought about the randy state of his dick. This had been the third time that week he'd woken with the desire to be fucked.

"Maybe I'll get away this weekend," Archer muttered as

he pushed from the bed. He headed toward the shower, his thoughts on his workload. "Never mind that." Archer shook his head. "No way that'll happen."

Resigning himself to more time with his own hand, Archer started the shower, then used the time it took to warm up to piss and brush his teeth. Stepping into the stall, Archer quickly cleaned up and mentally readied himself for another day.

As Archer shaved, he thought about the applications he'd received for deputies. He hadn't been all that thrilled with his prospects. Still, needing to please the mayor, he knew he needed to interview at least two of the guys.

The fact that the mayor's son—Darcy Loreman—was one of the applicants meant the man expected to be a shoe-in for the job.

Not happening.

Archer had spotted the notations in Darcy's file. The sheriff he currently worked under two towns over had remarked his bullying mentality. Darcy was also a bigot, and not just against homosexuals. Sheriff Colden had noticed excessive force against Hispanics and blacks, too.

When Darcy had graduated from the academy, there hadn't been an opening for a deputy in his town, and Archer was damn grateful for that. He had no intention of adding an asshole bully to his department.

No matter how much the mayor pressures me.

The sound of Archer's phone drew his attention. He turned off the faucet water, grabbed the hand towel from the rack, and started from the still-steamy bathroom. As he headed to his cell, he patted his freshly shaved face dry.

Placing the towel over his left shoulder, Archer picked up his phone with his right hand. He spotted the name on the screen and lifted his left brow. A call from his father was unexpected.

Marshal Montgomery had been the town's prior sheriff.

He'd retired six years ago, making way for Archer to be voted into the position. His support had probably been partly due to being his father's son.

"Hi, Dad," Archer greeted.

"Hello, son," Marshal responded. "How are you this morning? Didn't catch you on your way to the office, did I?"

"Just getting dressed," Archer told him as he crossed to his dresser and opened a drawer. He'd noticed a bit of tension in his father's voice and did his best not to scowl as he pulled out a pair of boxer-briefs. "Heading out in about forty minutes."

Archer knew his father was aware of what time he left for work, so he wondered at Marshal's comment.

"Good. Good."

Tucking his phone between his ear and his shoulder, Archer waited for more as he pulled on his underwear. He'd settled the elastic around his waist by the time he heard his father clear his throat. Knowing Marshal would get to it in his own time, Archer pulled a pair of nice jeans from the drawer and pulled them on, too.

While on occasion, Archer did need to wear dress slacks to the office, being in a small town, most of the time, it wasn't necessary.

"So, I hear you have a couple of openings for deputies."

When Marshal finally spoke, that wasn't what Archer had been expecting. Of course, he hadn't really known what to think. His father had raised him alone after Archer's mother had died when he'd been twelve.

"Yes, sir," Archer confirmed slowly, taking a white undershirt from his dresser. Fisting his hand in the fabric, he rested it on his hip. "Two, and I'm having a hell of a time with the applicants."

"Too many?" Marshal sounded hopeful.

Huh.

Archer shook his head even though he knew his father

wouldn't be able to see it. "Too few. Not too many people want to live way out here anymore."

Sometimes, rural ranch country had its drawbacks, too.

Marshal heaved a rough sigh. "Was afraid of that."

Narrowing his eyes, Archer cocked his head. "How'd you even hear about it, anyway?"

Growling came through the line. "Sheldon called me. Wanted me to put in a good word with you for his son."

Groaning, Archer settled on the side of his bed. "Damn mayor," he grumbled. "Of course, he did." Hearing Marshal's grunt of acknowledgment, Archer asked, "So, you gonna try to convince me to hire his son?"

Marshal snorted. "You should know me better than that. I was damn relieved when he graduated the academy and I'd already filled all my positions."

Archer nodded. His father had taught him his values. Measure a person's worth through their actions, regardless of skin tone, accent, religion, gender, or sexuality. He wanted his department to uphold those same statutes.

"So, suggestions?" Archer asked, trusting his father's intuition.

"Stall," Marshal offered. Fortunately, he wasn't done. "I'm putting out feelers with people I trust who are still on the force. Maybe we can drum up a few, much more worthy candidates."

While Archer had already been stalling and wasn't certain how much longer he could continue to do so—hell, his staff was burning the candle at both ends as it was, and a round of colds were going through them—he nodded anyway.

"Thanks, Dad. I appreciate it," he told the man who'd raised him. "I know the mayor wants his son and another guy from that same office to be hired. Guess they're friends. Cut from the same cloth." Leaving his shirt draped over his knee, he rubbed the back of his neck. "It'd be disastrous at the office to have to work with them, let alone for me to constantly monitor their actions."

"Agreed," his father replied. "I'll help where I can."

"Thanks, Dad," Archer repeated for want of something to say.

"Well, I better let you get on with your day," Marshal stated. "I'll keep you posted with what I find out."

"Have a great day, Dad," Archer told him, since he thought thanking him again would sound redundant.

"You, too, son," Marshal replied. "Stay safe."

"Yes, sir," Archer replied on reflex, then the line went dead. Placing his phone on the nightstand, he rose back to his feet. "Good grief," Archer grumbled, pulling his shirt over his head. "Who the fuck is lining Mayor Loreman's pockets?"

Archer had been discreetly looking into Mayor Sheldon Loreman's activities for years. So far, he'd never been able to find anything. He just knew he had to keep looking.

There was no way Sheldon could live the life of leisure and fund his last reelection campaign — two years prior — without some serious backing.

So who is it?

While Archer hoped his suspicion that Sheldon wasn't taking money from drug runners was correct, he feared he was right. His gut instinct normally was. There was just something slimy beneath Sheldon's oh-so-charming smile that made his stomach churn.

Pushing those thoughts from his mind, Archer finished dressing, tucking his sheriff's uniform shirt into his jeans. He couldn't do anything about it until he had a lead. So far, he hadn't been able to find one.

I'll find something soon.

Archer had to believe that. While drinking a cup of coffee, he whipped up a couple of scrambled eggs, and in bacon grease in another pan, he browned two no-grain English muffins. He grabbed a pair of the sausage patties he'd cooked several days before—using a pound of breakfast sausage to make many at the same time so he would have leftovers—and popped them into the microwave. Finally, Archer took a block of mild cheddar from his fridge and used his cheese slicer to cut off several thin pieces.

Within fifteen minutes, Archer had compiled a pair of sausage, egg, and cheese sandwiches. He wrapped one in parchment paper and placed it in his insulated lunch bag for later. After adding a snack baggie containing a couple servings of pecans as well as a container of sliced green bell peppers to the small cooler, his lunch was complete.

Then Archer headed to his table with his coffee and sandwich to enjoy his grain-free, low-carb breakfast. As he ate, he pulled up his work emails on his phone. He scrolled through them, scanning their contents, and mentally prioritized them for when he reached his office.

After finishing his food, Archer licked the forefingers of each hand before wiping them on a napkin. He headed to the kitchen and washed his hands. Finally, he tossed his paper plate and napkin into the garbage before a quick wash-up of the pans and utensils he'd used.

Archer took a quick look around, confirming that his kitchen and dining area had been put back to rights.

Clipping his phone to his belt, Archer headed back into his bedroom. He pulled the gun safe from his nightstand and opened it. Slipping his pistol into his holster, he checked over everything one more time.

Satisfied, Archer headed out the door to make the twenty-five minute drive into town for work.

Archer was just a few minutes from Main Street when his phone lit up, the trill of an incoming call sounding through his truck's speakers. Hitting a button on the wheel, he answered.

"Sheriff Montgomery."

"Hey, Sheriff, I'm sorry to bother you on your way in, but I needed to apprise you of a situation here at the station." The voice of Deputy Geraldo Martinez, his second-in-command and someone he considered a friend, came through his dash. "You may wanna pull over."

Concerned at how Geraldo pitched his voice low, Archer did as his friend suggested. He pulled over on the side of the road and put his truck in park. Then he removed his phone from the connection to the truck and lifted it to his ear.

"What's up, Gero? What's going on?"

Geraldo sighed through the line, then muttered, "Darcy is here looking for you. When I told him you weren't in and asked him what he needed, he told me he wanted to ask when his interview would be and when you would be in."

Heaving an annoyed sigh, Archer rubbed his forehead. "I see." He thought quickly, knowing Geraldo was waiting for instruction. "If you do me a solid and set him up with an appointment for Thursday at one-thirty, then get him to leave, I'll pick up your favorite coffee and muffin from Lacy's House of Beans."

Letting out a hum of pleasure, Geraldo smacked his lips exaggeratedly so it came through the line. "Coffee cake and a cappuccino on you? Oh, I can do that."

Smirking, Archer asked, "What are you going to tell Darcy, just in case it comes up later?"

Geraldo chuckled. "We cover a lot of rural ranches. You had a call come in to check out an issue at one of them." Snorting, he pointed out, "You know how long those can take. You never know when you'll get back in."

Archer bet Geraldo wore a shit-eating grin, and he guessed Darcy had said something not so respectful to Geraldo, who was clearly Hispanic. Considering his deputy was a damn fine officer, he couldn't give a shit about his heritage. He only cared about his work ethic, which was above reproach.

Yep. Don't want him anywhere near my department.

"Actually, I did have a call come in real early this morning . . . a little after three in the morning, but you'll probably want to check into this tonight," Geraldo told him, since he'd been covering the office over the night shift. "An anonymous tip came in about strange goings-on at Nicholas Lindson's ranch."

"Strange goings-on?" Archer couldn't help but tease. "Did they really say that?"

Geraldo chuckled. "Yep. A woman's voice, but she wouldn't give her name." Sobering, he told him, "She claims to have seen hulking men transporting a cougar, as if they were smuggling animals."

"Huh," Archer murmured. "After everything that's happened to that family, seems odd they'd—" Snapping his mouth shut, he bit back his musings. "Well, you're right. I'll check out your report and make a plan to do a little surveillance tonight."

"Damn," Geraldo grumbled. "Wish I wasn't on the night shift. I'd go with you."

"Sorry, man," Archer responded, taking on a commiserating tone. "As soon as I can find a couple more deputies I trust, I'll start taking some night shifts, too, and along with the others, we'll all start getting into a more regular schedule rotation."

Geraldo hummed. "Can't wait."

Neither could Archer.

CHAPTER TWO

Growling under his breath, Lludd banged out of the main ranch house. He knew that if it were possible, his medium-purple hide would be sporting a blush. As it was, he refused to think he felt hot for any other reason than his body seethed with indignant rage.

"Goddamned brother," Lludd grumbled on a snarl. "Smacking me upside the head like a youngling and telling me to cut out my shit and watch my mouth."

Lludd clenched his clawed hands, feeling the prick of them digging into his thick-hided palms. It wasn't as if he'd intended to offend Maggie when he'd commented that he could see her already expanding waistline even though she was only two months along. After all, some women just showed early.

That was life.

Besides, Lludd was actually happy for Maggie, the witch, and her bonded familiar, Sandra. They had used Nicholas's semen to artificially inseminate her. The pair were smart, kind, and were part of the ranch family.

He would never intentionally insult them.

At one time, Sandra had been betrothed to Nicholas Lindson, who happened to be his eldest brother's mate. Nicholas and Bodb had met and bonded right before the pair's wedding, so even though both were in relationships with someone else—someone of the same sex, and Sandra was in the closet and feared coming out—they had still wed. They'd never consummated it, and eventually, they'd chosen to get it annulled.

Sadly, Sandra had been correct, and she'd been disowned.

That didn't matter, though, because Sandra had them, those paranormals who made the ranch their home, a family of their own making.

Doesn't that mean I should have been cut a little slack? I'm an honorary brother, after all, even if I am a gargoyle.

Lludd had always been blunt to the point of rudeness. He didn't try to insult on purpose. Sometimes, he just didn't think about how his knee-jerk responses would sound out of his mouth.

He'd been living at the ranch for almost a year. Hadn't they learned that by now?

Remembering Maggie's cheeks turn bright red and the way Sandra growled and glared at him, Lludd did feel a measure of remorse.

Why were women so temperamental about their weight? It was just a body. Besides, a woman carrying young was gorgeous and glowing in a way one could hardly describe.

Maggie was gorgeous right now.

Lludd strode across the yard, his slate-gray wings wrapped around his shoulders. Deciding to make rounds to burn off some of his annoyance, he peered through the inky darkness of night. As a gargoyle, Lludd could easily discern everything around him.

The main driveway led into the massive gravel yard sporting plenty of parking. When coming in, the ranch home was off to the left. A good one hundred feet separated it from a large barn and a number of paddocks of varying sizes.

The barn was comprised of seven regular stalls, a wash rack, a large tack and grain room, and an office. For the most part, that was where Nicholas would meet clients. A sign on the drive indicated for visitors to inquire for help at the office. From what Lludd understood about the operation, someone was always on hand in or near that barn during business hours.

The surrounding paddocks all contained one or more loafing sheds depending on their sizes. Sometimes, horses were housed in them. If a buyer was expected, there could be dozens of cattle waiting in the larger of them.

Panning his gaze over the area, Lludd thought about heading down the driveway that ran between the house and the barn. Down that way were more of the same, each designated for something — foaling barns, training pens, paddocks, and arenas, as well as the areas used for mating their quarter horse stud. Near the back was the foreman's cabin — Stanley Redfeather's home — as well as the bunkhouse, which housed a half dozen or so others.

Lludd spotted movement out of the corner of his eye and turned his attention toward the barn. Seeing a shadow that didn't belong, he eased into the shadows and began making his way in that direction. He rounded the other side of the barn, listening and scenting carefully.

The scent of horses, manure, and hay flowed across Lludd's senses, and he realized he was upwind.

Damn.

Pausing at the corner of the back of the building, Lludd carefully peered around it. He was just in time to see a booted foot disappearing between the narrowly opened door. Narrowing his eyes, Lludd followed, fighting back a growl, letting out a low deep breath.

Some hand must be meeting another for a hook-up.

There was no other reason for one of their cowboys to be sneaking in the back of the barn at ten-thirty at night. Since these animals were all earmarked to be shown to a buyer over the next few days, no one was supposed to be in there other than the night watchman . . . and they didn't need to sneak.

Deciding to give the hand a scare — after all, rules were in place for a reason — the elder's safety — Lludd crept forward.

Lludd yanked open the door and snarled. "This barn is off-limits at this time of night," he roared, lifting his arms and wings, after all, all the hands knew of paranormals, including gargoyles. "Turn and declare yourself."

To Lludd's shock, the man who turned to face him was a stranger—and a handsome one at that. The guy wore faded jeans, boots, and a flannel shirt. His muscular frame stood around six-foot-one, and his black hat hid his face.

The gasp of shock and the acrid scent of fear, however . . . that Lludd didn't miss. Odd that he found some underlying masculine baseness to it pleasing. Except, just as his blood began to warm, the fear turned to an acidic smell of panic.

Fuck! What the hell? Was a hand meeting someone uninitiated? Bad, bad, bad.

Lludd began to lift his hands, opening his mouth to try to soothe. Whoever the guy was, he didn't want to hurt him. Unfortunately, the other man didn't seem to be of the same inclination.

As Lludd rumbled, "Easy, human," the stranger pulled a gun from somewhere behind his back.

Without a word, the human fired.

Pain flared through Lludd's upper right torso. The thick scent of his blood perfumed the air. His ears rang from the sound of the gunfire as well as the screaming whinnies of several frightened horses.

Lludd stumbled backward, struggling to form thoughts through the pain. Knowing he couldn't go down—*what if this man is actually after Bodb*—he drew on his millennia of warrior's training and pushed through it. Bending his knees and spreading his wings, Lludd lunged upward and forward. Seeing the trembling human swing his gun up and in his direction, he adjusted the angle of his wings and arced left, then right.

The *bang, bang* of the weapon caused his ears to continue to ring. A sting to his left side told him at least one of the man's bullets had nicked him.

Impressive.

Then Lludd was on the male. He grabbed the human's hand where he clutched the weapon. Pushing it upward toward the ceiling—*I'll have to confirm the hay in the loft doesn't end up on fire*—Lludd used his momentum to take the man to the ground.

Lludd wrapped his other arm around the human, cradling his head and neck. As annoyed as he was to be shot by the guy, he didn't want to hurt him. If the stranger was there to meet someone, it wasn't this man's fault that his date hadn't been waiting to soothe him.

Oddly, the thought of this human meeting another caused Lludd to growl softly.

"Oh, fuck!" the human cried. "I'm a dead man."

"You're not going to die, human," Lludd countered, even as he tugged the gun from his grip. "Just gonna meet a vampire next."

Ideally, having a stranger on the property would be an easy fix—one of their resident vampires could easily alter his memories.

Except, why the fuck did bile surge in his throat upon thinking about a vampire touching the human's mind. He inhaled deeply, trying to get his roiling emotions under control as he pinned the human to the barn's floor. Surely it was just because of the pain in his torso and side that was affecting him.

Wait.

While the smell of his blood perfumed the air, clogging his senses, something else managed to break through—an earthy, masculine goodness that he registered beneath the scent of fear and panic.

Once again, Lludd found his dick twitching.

As Lludd peered down at the man, confusion gave way to suspicion. He bent his arm and lowered his face, ignoring the way the guy cringed beneath his much bigger bulk. As Lludd took a deep inhale at the crook of the stranger's neck, he registered the pounding of booted feet outside the barn.

Mate!

The realization caused Lludd to rear up in shock, still half-crouching over the prone man.

"Damn," Lludd whispered in awe as he took in the gorgeous human sprawled beneath him. The man's chiseled features were on clear display since his hat had been knocked off—revealing wide green eyes with laugh lines to either side. A goatee framed his lips, and Lludd couldn't wait to feel that facial hair everywhere on his body. A shiver of need worked through him as Lludd murmured, "Delicious."

"Please don't eat me," the man whimpered.

"Eat you?" Lludd shook his head and frowned. "I wouldn't—"

"Lludd, let the sheriff up, please."

Snapping his attention to Nicholas, who spoke from a few feet away, Lludd stared at his brother's mate. He froze, not wanting to release the man who was the other half of his soul. This guy—the sheriff—was everything to him.

Nicholas gave him a slight smile. "You did your job. You stopped the intruder." Indicating the downed sheriff, he added, "We'll take it from here."

Take it from here.

Those words caused his blood to freeze in his veins. He knew what they meant. It had been his own plan moments before—turn the human over to a vampire to have his memory wiped.

"No," Lludd rumbled. Lowering his bulk, he crouched protectively over his mate.

"Lludd." Bodb stepped up beside Nicholas. Even in his human form, his brother struck an intimidating figure. Holding Lludd's gaze in a steady gaze, Bodb ordered, "Lludd, rise and come to me."

Unable to deny the order of an elder—even if he was his

brother—Lludd slowly rose to his feet. He glanced down at the sheriff once, sweeping his gaze appreciatively over his masculine form, then headed toward his brother. Meeting Bodb's eyes, he spotted the way his brother swept his gaze over him, concern in his expression.

That was when the pain returned, the scent of his blood flooding his nostrils once more, since he was no longer close to the heady smell of his mate.

Bodb gripped his left shoulder and guided him out of the barn. "Tell me what happened quickly," his brother urged. "I don't see an exit wound on that upper torso shot, and we need to get the bullet out."

"I spotted movement at the edge of the barn," Lludd rumbled, glancing back at the barn's doorway even as he allowed Bodb to lead him away. Then he spotted Spieron—one of their resident vampires, this one bonded with Nicholas's father, Albert—jogging toward the barn. Lludd gripped to his brother's forearm in a tight hold. "Please, brother. Don't erase the sheriff's mind. Please."

"Why would you—"

Lludd didn't normally interrupt his brother, seeing as he was an elder and all, but his urgency forced more words out of his throat. "Please, Bodb. I'll go to Virgil without question as long as you vow to share about paranormals with the human. Make him understand we're not a threat." Lludd could feel the loss of blood catching up with him, and he felt his mind begin to spin a little. Forcing himself to continue to hold Bodb's gaze, Lludd squeezed his brother's forearm. "He's mine."

Bodb's eyes widened for an instant before he snapped his focus to Spieron who was about to disappear into the barn. "Spieron, hold up," he called before refocusing on Lludd. "I'll take care of it." Bodb smirked. "At least the basics." Then his brother released him and hustled toward the waiting vampire.

Relief flooding him, Lludd turned and headed in the other direction. As much as he wanted to return to his mate's side, he knew he couldn't. His brother spoke words of wisdom.

Lludd needed to get the bullet removed before his accelerated healing trapped it in his body. That meant getting to Virgil. The cougar shifter was their ranch's on-hand medic. In a prior life, he'd been a doctor in a little hospital in some wayside, seaside village.

"You look like you could use a hand."

Registering Stanley standing next to him, Lludd realized the foreman was even gripping his upper arm. "Come on, Lludd," the big Native American urged, wrapping his arm around his waist. "Let's get you to Virgil. You'll feel better shortly."

Lludd nodded, seeing the wisdom in that. "Thanks." After all, the sooner he could heal safely, the sooner he could find out more about his mate and pursue him.

"Who'd you snag in the barn?" Stanley asked softly, perhaps giving him something to focus on other than the pain in his chest and side. "How'd you end up shot?"

Grunting, Lludd admitted, "Thought it was one of ours planning to use the barn as a hook-up spot." Wincing since he denoted that meant he didn't trust those on the ranch, he muttered, "Sorry. Um, was wrong. Nicholas called the human I'd caught the sheriff."

"Damn," Stanley muttered, shaking his head. "Bummer for him." Giving him a side-eyed smirk, he added, "And don't feel too bad about your assumption. If I'd seen a cowboy figure slipping into the barn, I woulda thought the same thing . . . and planned to ream him over the coals for allowing himself to think with his dick."

"Never see you hookin' up," Lludd commented absently.

His head swam a little, and he knew he leaned heavily on the human. "Damn, you're strong."

Stanley chuckled huskily into his ear. "Thanks, big guy. And I don't hook up with people at the ranch." With a shrug of his shoulder, he claimed, "I used to, but it made for an awkward working environment once when the other guy got clingy, so I stopped. I'll find the one someday."

"Good for you," Lludd rumbled. "I just found mine."

Hissing in a sharp breath, Stanley asked, "Sheriff Montgomery?"

Lludd wasn't sure if his mate was the same sheriff, so he shrugged. "If it's the same guy in the barn." He smiled, even as his vision blurred. "He's the one. My mate."

Huh. Is my voice slurring?

Then a thud sounded, but he couldn't seem to focus on it. He vaguely recognized Stanley's shout as he heard him call for Virgil. The cougar shifter ordered him to be laid on the bed, and Virgil's shifter mate said he would get supplies.

When did I enter a bedroom?

A second later, Lludd couldn't seem to keep his eyelids open any longer.

CHAPTER THREE

H*oly shit! I'm not dead.*
Archer watched in shock as Bodb led the creature away . . . and not even with a leash. He spoke, and the beast obeyed as if he completely understood. Bodb even put his hand on his shoulder and guided him out the door as if it were nothing.

Not until they'd both disappeared out the door did Archer register the hand held out to him. Snapping his focus from the doorway and the couple of people standing there, he peered up at Nicholas. The ranch owner gazed upon him steadily, no fear or concern in his eyes or expression at all.

Nicholas wiggled his fingers. "Come on, Sheriff. Let me help you up."

Reaching up, Archer took the man's hand, and Nicholas easily hefted him to his feet. He gripped Archer's other upper arm with his free hand, helping him get his balance. It took him a moment to stop the swaying, and he knew it must be caused by shock.

Really, though, what did a person expect? He'd just been jumped by something that looked an awful lot like the infamous Jersey Devil. The beast had wings and claws and fangs and pointed teeth and everything.

"Sheriff Montgomery?" Nicholas squeezed his upper arm while releasing his other arm's hand. "You with me?"

"So the tip was true," Archer muttered, scowling at Nicholas. "You're in exotic animal trafficking now? What the hell was that thing?" Pulling away, Archer glanced around warily, suddenly realizing how outnumbered he was and that he was no longer armed.

"Relax." Nicholas lifted his hands in placation. "We're not in animal trafficking, and you're completely safe here. I promise."

Albert, Nicholas's father—although he'd been known as his uncle for decades—stepped forward and held out Archer's hat. "Here you go, Sheriff." Then Albert pointed to the left. "And your weapon is there. Feel free to grab it, if it'll make you feel better. None of us touched it."

Still eyeing everyone warily, Archer did just that. "If you're not in animal trafficking, then I need to see a permit on . . . whatever the fuck that was." As he spoke, he slid his weapon into his holster, but he left the guard unlatched.

Nicholas nodded. "Okay." He pointed toward the doorway at the man approaching the barn. "Let me introduce you to Spieron. He'll be able to explain so much better than I can."

Just as the muscular, auburn-haired male reached the doorway, Bodb's voice came from outside. "Spieron. Hold up."

Spieron glanced Archer's way but did as the other man bid.

Bodb appeared behind him, and they both entered. "I'm afraid I'm going to have to take point on this explanation, Spieron. Sorry we called you when you weren't needed."

"Really? You sure?" Spieron's brows lifted a little. A second later, he dipped his head in a barely-there nod before saying, "Of course. Sorry." His lips quirked in a smile as he headed toward Albert. "And joining my man is never a hardship."

"What's up, Bodb?" Nicholas asked, drawing closer to his lover. "Is Lludd okay? Did you get him to Virgil already?"

"I left that duty to Stanley," Bodb stated, wrapping his arm around Nicholas's waist and tucking him close. "Lludd needed me to stop Spieron's explanation, so we could tell him the truth."

Bodb widened his brown eyes in some meaningful way that Nicholas obviously understood, because his lips parted in surprise. "Oh."

Archer really didn't like the sound of that. "Just what was Spieron supposed to do to me?" he growled, reaching for his weapon again. "What the fuck are you all into?"

After all the scandals that had involved this family, he should have known something hinky was going on. Nicholas had married Sandra. Then less than a year later, they'd had it annulled. They'd come out as both having completely separate relationships with someone of the same sex.

Considering the fact that Sandra had immediately been cut off by her family, her hiding her sexuality had been a little understanding. Then, quite a bit of change-out of hands, combined with the bringing in of bruiser-sized men to the ranch, made Archer think Bodb—whose last name he couldn't recall hearing—was some bigwig in hiding. Finally, there had been the tales that spread like wildfire through town about how Nicholas's mother had had an affair with Albert, then passed him off as her husband's firstborn, who was Baltus, Albert's older brother.

Talk about a messed up heritage.

Archer had thought they'd finally begun settling down to the quiet life with the family of their own making.

Guess I was wrong.

"Whoa, now, Sheriff." Spieron obviously caught on to Archer's irritation, for he actually urged his much larger partner behind him. With his other hand, he held up his hand. "Like Nicholas said, you're perfectly safe."

Nicholas scoffed as he scowled at Bodb. "You gave him the wrong idea, my love."

Bodb sighed, his expression turning pained. "Sorry, Sheriff." Taking a step backward, he indicated the door. "Please, come up to the ranch house with us. We'll explain what Lludd is and why you're not in danger here."

Archer nodded slowly, still on edge. "You all walk in front. I'll follow."

"Fair enough," Nicholas stated, urging Bodb to turn. "Let's go."

After Bodb and Nicholas filed out of the barn, Spieron started after them. When he noticed Albert lingering, he cocked his head. "Beloved?"

Albert indicated the barn. "I need to walk the line of the horses and check over them all." He pointed skyward. "Then I gotta crawl into the loft and make certain none of those bullets threw off sparks that started a fire." Grimacing, Albert focused on Nicholas. "It's the dry season. Better safe than sorry."

Wincing, Archer nodded. "Right."

Spieron moved away from the door, starting toward the first stall. "I'll assist."

After another wary look at the pair who began to check things out, Archer left the barn. He glanced around quickly. For an instant, he thought about trying to run.

Two things stopped him. First, Bodb and Nicholas stood halfway between the barn and the house, staring and waiting expectantly. They had a pair of men with them that, while dressed like cowboys, screamed security. Second, if Archer ran, he knew he wouldn't get any answers.

Taking a slow deep breath, Archer headed to the ranch house.

When Archer reached the porch and climbed the steps, he spotted the smirk on the dark-haired male's lips. "Welcome to the rabbit hole, Alice." He waggled his brows, and his brown eyes twinkled.

"You're not helping, Sindrid," Bodb commented dryly, leading the way inside.

"Sorry, sir," the man—Sindrid—replied automatically, but

he still wore an unabashed grin.

Oddly enough, something about the friendly man's smile put Archer at ease more than either of Nicholas or Bodb's reassurances. "So, the rabbit hole," he murmured, narrowing his eyes at Sindrid. "Is this where you offer the red or blue pill?"

Sindrid grinned at him. "Naw, man. You already took the red pill, because you met Lludd."

"I was investigating a tip," Archer claimed defensively. "Someone says you're smuggling exotic animals, and now I see why."

"I would really like to know who gave you that tip," the other bodyguard-like man stated. He held out his hand. "I'm Ssimeas, by the way."

Archer took the big black man's hand, giving it a quick shake. After releasing it, he pointed his finger at him. "You're the one who took Attain off the market."

Ssimeas nodded as he grinned broadly, flashing even white teeth. "Yep. That's me." He sounded extremely pleased with himself.

"Sindrid, go raid the snacks in the side-bar in the dining room, and bring us some refreshment to the family room," Bodb ordered as they strode through a huge dining space with a long wooden table that sat a dozen easy. He pointed at a wide sideboard with a couple of mini-fridges under it. "I'm in the mood for a couple of crème puffs and strawberry canapes."

"Oh, and the sausage pastries," Nicholas added as he followed Bodb toward a pair of sliding doors to the right.

As Archer followed slowly, he found his mouth watering. He didn't eat that kind of thing often, but if he was about to learn something life-altering, maybe a treat was in order. Of course, he'd have to find time to hit the hiking trails to burn off all those empty carbs in the next day or so.

At forty-two, Archer found he had to work harder to stay fit. He'd seen his father's figure start to go around this time, so he'd changed his diet when he hit forty to curb the possibility. So far, it had worked, and he was pleased he still sported a six-pack.

I'll wait until I hear what this rabbit hole is all about.

"Want a drink, Sheriff?" Nicholas asked as he headed to a bar off to the right of the room. "Alcohol or not, I probably have it."

Okay. That he couldn't resist, especially after the shock he'd had that evening.

"You have a decent scotch back there?"

Nicholas nodded. "Ice?"

Archer shook his head.

"Have a seat," Bodb ordered, waving his hand to indicate the assortment of comfortable sofas and chairs. "I'm not certain how long this will take."

"You don't?" Archer headed to a reclining chair and eased onto it. He gripped the arms, marveling at the comfort. Pushing aside his distraction, Archer returned his focus to Bodb. "Why?"

"Because it always depends on how accepting the human is," Bodb replied enigmatically.

Before Archer could question that odd answer, Nicholas approached him with his drink. He quickly took the tumbler, since he was balancing a beer bottle and a tumbler of clear fluid with his other hand. After bringing it to his nose, he sniffed and couldn't help but hum appreciatively.

"Thank you," Archer murmured before taking a sip. The rich liquid burned just a smidge as it went down. "Nice."

As Sindrid rolled a cart full of an assortment of finger foods into the room, Ssimeas took a seat on a nearby couch. A bottle of beer in his right hand and some kind of pastry in his left. Bodb cleared his throat, getting Archer's attention.

"So, the first thing you should know is that Lludd is *not* an animal. Lludd is a sentient paranormal creature called a gargoyle."

Archer stared at Bodb, holding his gaze . . . waiting for the punch line. When nothing else was forthcoming, he oh-so-eloquently stated, "Huh?"

Nicholas leaned forward from where he sat next to Bodb on the small sofa. Holding his beer between his palms, he stated, "So, look. Paranormals are sentient beings that live on earth right along with humans. They are born, work, find love, raise a family, and die just like us." He waved one palm at Bodb. "Bodb is also a gargoyle, but since he mated with me, he can take on a human form. Lludd is not mated, yet, so you saw him in his true form." Straightening, Nicholas added, "I don't want to overwhelm you, but there are many other species of paranormals out there, too. Those myths about werewolves and vampires and magick *did* come from somewhere, you know."

Archer's mind spun as he processed Nicholas's words. Lifting his drink, he frowned into the liquid before taking a sip. He took a second drink, buying time.

If what they were saying was true . . .

"I just shot a person, not an animal?" Archer's gut churned as unease slithered up his spine. Meeting Bodb's solemn gaze, he whispered, "Didn't I?"

Bodb offered one slow nod. "You did. You shot my baby brother." His nostrils flared as he added, "He's one of the guards here, because I am an elder of our race."

Archer bobbled the glass as he reared back in his seat hard enough that he nearly toppled the reclining chair when it began to swivel. Letting out an unmanly *eep*, he managed to get himself and the chair under control.

Sindrid chuckled softly. "That chair swivels so it can be turned to face that way, because a screen can be lowered from the ceiling to watch movies." He pointed behind Archer.

Too afraid to glance in that direction, Archer just nodded. "I fired my service weapon on someone," he murmured, shaking his head. "I hit him, too. I saw the blood. Smelled it." Groaning, Archer grumbled, "Gonna have to write up a report for the shots fired. Gonna—" He paused shaking his head. "How am I gonna explain—" Then Archer snapped his attention back to Bodb. "Will Lludd be okay?"

While Archer's mind spun crazily, like a wheel stuck in sand that couldn't find traction, he knew that was the most important thing.

Bodb nodded once. "I received a text from Virgil while heading in here. He lost a lot of blood, but he'll survive." His smile turned kind. "Don't worry. He won't hold it against you. He'll probably turn up at your place to apologize, at some point."

Archer gaped at Bodb. "H-He would c-come to my house? Why?" Then he shook his head since that wasn't the most important thing. "Why would he apologize? *I* shot *him*."

Nicholas shrugged. "You were acting in self-defense because you thought your life was threatened." Waving vaguely in the direction of the barn. "Not the best way to be introduced to paranormals, but you seem to be taking it pretty well."

"Uh, I'm pretty sure I'm going to freak out as soon as I get home," Archer admitted. He knew himself. His heart still hammered wildly in disbelief, and he wanted to deny, deny, deny. Except, he knew what he'd seen, what he'd experienced. "I-I guess I should come up with some questions, but my mind is kinda blank." Although, not of everything . . ."Why did Lludd ask you to explain and not Spieron?"

Grimacing, Nicholas rubbed the back of his neck and looked away.

Bodb sighed deeply, but he answered, "Spieron is a vampire. He has the ability to alter the memories of most humans." His expression turned kind as he claimed, "He would have searched your mind for the reason you were there, then input memories that would give you a plausible narrative." After a second of hesitation, Bodb added, "And he would make you forget meeting Lludd."

Archer's breathing sped up, turning to pants. Black spots danced across his vision. He couldn't seem to get enough air into his lungs.

"Head between your knees," a deep voice ordered as a hand landed on the back of Archer's neck. "Bend forward."

Doing anything other than what the hand on him urged him would have been impossible. Whoever gripped him was way too strong. He found his head thrust between his knees as another hand stroked up and down his back soothingly.

Then the oddest thing happened.

Archer felt a body press close against his side, and a strange vibrating sensation flowed through him. A low rumble accompanied it, and he found himself relaxing. His body even began to sag against whoever held him.

"There ya go, Sheriff," the man rumbled. "You'll be okay. Everything will be fine."

Turning his head, Archer realized his chest was being cradled against Sindrid's side. Ssimeas stood on his other side, and he was rubbing his back. Nicholas and Bodb looked on in concern.

"So much for not freaking out until I got home," Archer muttered, embarrassment flooding him.

Chapter Four

"So Archer freaked out." Lludd sat heavily on the side of the bed.

His chest still hurt, but he was well on the mend. The bullet that had grazed his side was all but already healed. What ached the most was the fact that his mate was no longer on the property.

"Yes, but he was calm when he went home," Bodb assured him, sitting on his left.

Lludd nodded slightly. "If I visited, would he talk to me?"

Now that Lludd had scented his mate, he would be able to follow Archer's delicious aroma anywhere. His kind were excellent trackers due to the hundreds of extrasensory taste buds on his tongue. They were designed to practically taste the air.

"I'd give him a day," Nicholas urged, his smile turning commiserating. "Let him decompress for twenty-four hours. It'll also give you the chance to heal up." With a wink, he added, "Then take him something as an offering."

Cocking his head, Lludd squinted at Bodb's mate. "Like flowers?" he asked dubiously. "Do men like to be given flowers?"

Nicholas shrugged. "Some do, but no. I don't think Archer is the type." He shoved his hands into his pockets and leaned against the wall. "We'll have to think of something else."

"And for the love of all the gods," Bodb grumbled. "Try to think before you speak."

Lludd scowled. "If my mate is perfect for me, shouldn't he

want me just as I am?" He started to cross his arms over his chest, but the tug on his torso made him think better of it. "You didn't ask Nicholas to stop with his plans to get married to Sandra."

With a growl, Bodb muttered, "That's different."

"How?" Lludd asked. He didn't get it.

"Yeah, babe." Nicholas smirked. "How *is* that different?"

Bodb rolled his eyes. "I'm the paranormal. As the paranormal, it's my job to make you happy and take care of you."

"Marrying Sandra didn't make me happy," Nicholas pointed out, although his expression did soften. "But we did what needed to be done." Then Nicholas focused on Lludd. "I agree that if someone won't accept you for who you are, then they're not worth your time, but you do need to remember a few things, okay?"

Lludd nodded slowly, then shook his head. "What things?"

"Archer's human, and he's just had his world rocked," Nicholas warned him. "While we explained why secrecy and anonymity are so important, he agreed to never tell a soul, but we didn't get around to telling him about mates." Pulling his hands from his pockets, Nicholas spread them and lifted his shoulders in a beseeching way. "Since you weren't there, and the way he learned about us bred fear" — he grimaced and stared at the ceiling — "especially when I shared how Spieron could have completely altered his memory, with his panic attack, we didn't want to overload him —"

"Are you going somewhere with this?" Lludd grumbled, resting his clawed hands on his thighs.

"Right, right." Nicholas bobbed his head and hummed. "What I mean to say is, take it slow. Drop in during the evening and take him dinner. I hear he works late, because his department is shorthanded," he explained. "And we learned he likes to eat low-carb and grain-free. He didn't touch the pastries and canapes, but he loved the cheese and prosciutto rolls."

"Wait." Lludd held up his hand. "What's that even mean?"

"Which part?" Nicholas asked slowly, cocking his head.

"I get low-carb, but what's grain-free?" As a gargoyle, Lludd had never had to watch what he ate or worried about working out to stay fit. His body processed things so swiftly that he'd never had an issue. "Is he worried about his body? Is he sick?"

That would mean they should bond as swiftly as possible, so Lludd's superior genetics could strengthen his mate's.

"Well, Archer's a human in his early forties in a physically demanding job," Nicholas explained. "So yeah, he works hard to stay in shape. And I guess grain-free is not eating things made of things like wheat or corn or barley or oats. You know . . . a grain plant that has to be processed and cooked in some manner in order for a human to digest it."

"Huh," Lludd mumbled. "Didn't know that was a thing." Then discomfort hit him. "Do you think he'll expect me to eat that way? Because I don't know if I could give up bear claws."

For his mate, could he give up his favorite pastry?

Ugh!

Nicholas cocked his head. "Uh, no way to know that unless you sit down and have a frank discussion about it." He waved his hand at Lludd's body as he stated, "Explaining that paranormals process things so much faster, so they need more calories, would probably be enough to ease his worries about you becoming sick." Then a soft chuckle escaped Nicholas. "And the fact that you've been feeding yourself for over a thousand years without issue."

"Who knows, Lludd," Bodb cut in. "Maybe he'll loosen up his own restrictions once he realizes his body won't deteriorate the way an average human would over the years."

Lludd nodded, but he didn't want to ask his human to

change any more than he wanted to have to jump through hurdles to win his mate.

Huh. That was probably a selfish thought.

Blowing out a breath, Lludd slowly lowered to the bed. He was in a room in the bunkhouse that acted as an infirmary. Having lived over a millennium, he figured he would be slow to adjust.

But I will.

"Finding a mate and building a life together is a learning experience for everyone."

Upon hearing Ssimeas's voice, Lludd turned his head and spotted the medium-blue-skinned gargoyle leaning against the doorframe. He saw the understanding look on his face. His thick lips were quirked up at the corner, and his deep gray eyes twinkled.

"Remember when I wooed Attain? I drove him nuts," Ssimeas said with a laugh. "We could always send him gifts at his office."

Lludd cocked his head. "I thought you did that to let everyone know Attain was attached, because his father was trying to pair him with some chick."

Ssimeas grinned widely, showing off his pointed teeth. "It was still fun."

"Well, since he's low-carb, he won't eat much in the way of chocolates or most fruits," Nicholas pointed out, shaking his head. "And he's no-grain, so no cookies or donuts or brownies."

Shaking his head, Lludd muttered, "Then we'd be back to flowers."

Still grinning, Ssimeas stated, "Naw, that just means we need to get creative."

"We?" Lludd stared at Ssimeas. "What do you mean?"

"Dude!" Sindrid appeared behind Ssimeas's shoulder. "We're all gonna help. You only get one mate, and we all want you happy." He waggled his eyebrows. "And well-sexed."

Bodb groaned. "I do *not* want to hear about my brother's sex life."

"Why?" Lludd's other older brother—the middle one, Gladstone—grinned over the shoulders of the other pair in the doorway. He rested his forearms on one shoulder of each and leaned against them. "You always tried to weasel info about me and Dayvid's sex life." Gladstone waggled his black brow ridges. "How is this different?"

Placing his hands over his face, Bodb groaned. "I was young! That was four hundred years ago." He lifted his head and glared at their brother. "Why can't you let this go?"

Nicholas cackled with laughter. Bending over at the waist, he shook his head. A second later, tears dripped from his eyes.

"Nicholas?" Even Bodb sounded confused. "Is something wrong?" He went to his mate and rested his hand on his human's back, rubbing lightly. "My mate?"

Straightening enough to meet Bodb's gaze, Nicholas grinned broadly at him. "You guys." His eyes gleamed with humor. "You're what? Twelve hundred plus years at your last guess? Isn't that what you told me?"

Bodb nodded, still sporting a confused expression.

Nicholas snorted as he shook his head. Resting his hand on Bodb's arm, he straightened. "So, four hundred years ago, you were in your eight-hundreds, right?" At Bodb's continued nodding, Nicholas pointed out, "So you just called yourself young at eight hundred years old."

"Uhhhh . . ." Bodb seemed at a loss for words.

Gladstone chuckled. "Your man's got ya there." He winked. "We haven't been considered young in a long damn time."

Heaving a breath, Bodb wrapped an arm around Nicholas's waist and tugged him close to his side. The human pressed against him without a hint of resistance.

Lludd wondered if he would ever have that with Archer.

"So, not tonight, but tomorrow night," he began slowly. "I should take him food. Uh . . . something low-carb without grain."

"Spaghetti," Ssimeas stated, nodding sagely. "While it's not terribly low-carb with the tomato sauce and spaghetti, it's filling and can be reheated, making great leftovers." With a wide smile, he stated, "When he reheats it for lunch the next day, he'll be thinking of you."

"Uh, that's not grain-free," Nicholas pointed out. "Pasta, remember?"

Ssimeas's eyes widened. "Oh, not what I meant. Not that kind of spaghetti." Turning his attention to Lludd, he corrected, "Instead of pasta, use buttered spaghetti squash as the noodles. Add in olives and mushrooms, a few seasonings, and it'll be delicious."

Gladstone hummed, rubbing his chin. "What kind of meat does he prefer? Burger? Pork? Lamb? Meatballs?"

"How the hell am I supposed to know?" Lludd grumbled in irritation. "I've hardly met the man."

"Just thinkin' out loud, little bro," Gladstone told him. Glancing around, he asked, "Didn't Virgil have a run-in with him a couple of months back? At the bar, remember?"

"Yeah," Nicholas confirmed. "When he took his mate, Shaw, to Landry's bar and that asshole Henry tried to attack him. What are you thinking?"

"Well, Virgil knows Landry pretty well, and it seems Landry is on good terms with Archer." Gladstone shrugged. "Maybe Landry can help. Or at least, tell us who could."

"Where's Virgil?" Lludd asked. He hadn't seen the cougar shifter since he'd woken up. Biscane — a fellow unmated gargoyle — had been at his side.

Nicholas yawned before saying, "Asleep, which is where I need to be. I have a meeting with a potential buyer for that sorrel mare in" — he glanced at his phone, probably checking the time, and groaned—"less than five hours."

Lludd winced. "Sorry to cause such upheaval tonight."

Scoffing, Nicholas shook his head. "Don't—" Another yawn interrupted him.

Chuckling, Bodb grabbed him and slung him over his shoulder. "Time for bed, my mate."

With a laugh, Nicholas cried, "Not complaining about the bed but"—he smacked Bodb's ass as his eldest brother moved past those who made room around the doorway—"I could walk."

"Sure, you could," Bodb replied, his voice fading. "But then I couldn't do this."

The sound of a smack reached Lludd's ears, then the sound of Nicholas's growl. He didn't really sound upset, though.

Lludd shook his head before returning his attention to Gladstone, Sindrid, and Ssimeas. All three mated gargoyles peered at him with similar looks of sympathy and encouragement.

"You'll woo him, Lludd," Sindrid claimed with a nod.

"Yep." Ssimeas winked. "We're all in your corner. Don't you worry."

Gladstone winked. "And if something comes up and you say something offensive, we've all had plenty of time to learn the best ways to grovel at our mates' feet for forgiveness." Then Gladstone clapped Ssimeas on his shoulder and shook him from side to side a little. "Well, most of us, but I think this one could probably help in his own way, too."

Ssimeas barked a laugh even as he nodded. "Thanks, man." Clapping his hands, he stated, "Okay, while you sleep the day away and recover, we'll talk to Pauline about that low-carb spaghetti meal."

With a rakish grin, Sindrid added, "We'll be sure to have it ready at sunset, so you can hot-foot it right over there first thing after roost." Then he waved and turned away with

Ssimeas following.

His brother paused long enough to tell him, "And we'll discover his address and map a safe route to it." As he closed the behind him, he ordered, "Get plenty of rest, brother."

In the next moment, Lludd was left alone. Seeing as he was still exhausted and he'd been relieved of his duties, he did just that. Lludd swung his legs up, reclined on the mattress, and relaxed.

Lludd hoped he would see his mate in his dreams.

True to his brother and friends' words, as soon as Lludd woke from roost that evening, the fragrant scent of spaghetti hit his nostrils. He pushed off the bed—he couldn't remember the last time he'd reclined as a stone statue on a bed for the day—and headed out of the room. His body ached a little, but overall he felt pretty good.

Lludd headed to the nearest bunkhouse bathroom first. He went through his morning routine, showering and cleaning up, then reached into a basket under the sink and pulled out a fresh loincloth. Seeing as a number of gargoyles either lived in the bunkhouse or used the facilities to clean up daily, clean loincloths were always made available.

Sindrid, Ssimeas, and Gladstone—plus their mates—used large second-story suites. Lebone lived in a suite in the main house off the kitchen, since his mate, Pauline, was the ranch chef and housekeeper. Lludd and Biscane—as the last un-mated gargoyles—normally roosted in the hayloft of the barn.

Well, hopefully, I won't be doing that for much longer.

After the hot water of the shower, even Lludd's stiff muscles felt loose and comfortable. While the wound on his upper right pectoral would take a few days longer to heal, he wasn't in danger of tearing it open or anything. If he'd been human, the wound would have looked around four weeks old already.

Lludd headed to the open concept kitchen, dining, and living room space, and spotted his buddies as well as Virgil, Shaw, and Stanley. Seeing as sunset was around eight-thirty, he figured the other wranglers had already retreated to their rooms to enjoy their own pursuits or had gone into town.

"Hey, there's the lucky gargoyle," Gladstone greeted, heading toward him. "Have we got news for you."

Then Gladstone led Lludd to the dining room table. He pointed out the map of the area and what they'd learned of Archer over the course of the day.

CHAPTER FIVE

Archer groaned as he dragged his ass out of his pick-up, up his walk, and into his house. After worrying himself to death about the gargoyle he'd injured, he'd only made it to sleep in the wee hours of the morning. Then, to his ever-loving shock, Archer had dreamed about the creature . . . and it wasn't a PG dream by any means.

Waking up hard enough to pound nails hadn't happened to Archer since he was a teenager. He'd jacked off in damn near the shortest amount of time possible. If he was thinking about touching the gargoyle's dark-gray wings while doing it, well, he would never tell.

His day had gotten worse from there. He'd had to write up a report about his findings at the ranch — every word a lie, which made his coffee sour in his stomach. Then Mayor Loreman had called, asking why his son didn't have an interview until Thursday, even though that was the very next day. Finally, they'd received another anonymous tip about the ranch.

Someone was obviously pissed about some activity at the ranch, but without knowing the identity of the caller, Archer wasn't certain in what direction to look — Nicholas's incarcerated mother, someone from Sandra or Nicholas's high society past, or maybe even an old ranch hand upset about being let go.

Just what the fuck is going on?

One thing was for certain — Archer would have to make another trip out there. The idea caused both a fissure of unease

37

to travel down his spine as well as a flutter of excited butter-flies in his stomach. He figured the former reaction was normal after what he'd just learned. The latter . . . he couldn't explain in the least—the near wet dream aside.

Placing his keys on a hook of the key rack hanging near the front door, Archer moved slowly through the darkened foyer, then through the living space. He didn't bother turning on a light until he hit the dining room. Heading to the fridge, he grimaced as he thought about what to make for supper.

While his stomach grumbled, Archer had no energy for anything involved. He pulled out a carton of eggs and a package of bacon bits. Then he grabbed a small block of goat cheese.

"Bacon and eggs it is," Archer muttered as he set everything on the counter. As Archer reached for the frying pan in the drying rack, the soft rap of someone knocking on his back door caught his attention. "What the hell?"

Archer wasn't expecting anyone, and he couldn't remember the last time someone had dropped by unannounced.

Plus, the back door?

Then Archer recalled Bodb's words about Lludd possibly dropping by to apologize.

He really wouldn't . . . would he?

As Archer stood frozen in indecision, he heard the rap come once again.

Pulling his head out of his ass, Archer eased his way to his back door. He turned on the back patio light and eased the vertical slats of the blinds aside a little. Archer just managed to keep himself from stepping back in shock.

Archer thought he'd been prepared. Really, he had. Except, he wasn't.

Upon him seeing the massive creature known as Lludd, once more, Archer's heart rate spiked. His mouth dried, and his breathing sped up. Even with that reaction, he couldn't deny the heat that sizzled in his veins, too.

So fucking weird.

Peering at him from beneath the brim of a broad-brimmed cowboy hat, Lludd eyed him through the glass of the sliding door. He slowly lifted his hand and placed it on the pane. Instead of tapping it with his dark-gray claw-tipped appendages, he just rested his hand there.

"Archer," Lludd called through the glass.

While his voice sounded deep and soft, Archer still heard it.

"Will you let me in, Archer?" Lludd requested. "I would like to talk to you." After a heartbeat, two, where Archer still couldn't find his voice, Lludd pointed downward. "I brought dinner."

That shocked Archer out of his stupor. "You brought me dinner?"

Lludd nodded, his lips curving into a small smile. While most of his pointed teeth were not on display, his canines still slid over his lips. He finally tapped the glass with his claw.

"Please, Archer. Let me in."

Reaching down, Archer picked up the piece of wood from the track. The lock on the glass door was flimsy, after all. This way, if an intruder wanted in, they would have to break the pane.

Archer set it aside, unlocked the crappy lock, then pulled the door open. "Uh, hi. Lludd?"

Lame!

Lludd grinned, seeming pleased. "Yes."

Even seeing the male's sharp teeth, Archer knew the racing of his pulse wasn't caused by fear. He cleared his throat and took a step backward. "Um, please, come in."

After bending down, Lludd hefted a padded bag into his hands.

Then . . . Archer found a gargoyle in his home.

Rubbing the back of his neck, Archer indicated the kitchen counter to his left. "Uh, that was very thoughtful of you." After the gargoyle moved past him, going where he'd been bidden, Archer closed and locked the door again, although he didn't replace the wooden dowel.

Oh. Is it wise to lock myself in with a gargoyle?

Turning back, Archer looked over the male. Lludd hadn't just stopped at the bar. He'd moved around it and into the kitchen. One after another, he was opening cupboards.

"Is there something I can help you find?" Archer couldn't help but ask.

Right. He said he brought dinner.

Archer found his heart warm a bit at the gesture. He couldn't remember the last time someone had brought him a meal, especially one that smelled so amazing. Even through the sides of the warming bag, he could smell rich tomato sauce and something else.

Damn. Is that something Italian? I can't remember the last time I indulged in Italian.

His stomach rumbled in response to the aromas.

Lludd turned as he pulled out a pair of bowls—evidently, he'd found what he wanted—and moved toward him. "It does smell good, huh?" Placing them on the counter beside the bag, he grinned. "I'm hungry, too." Then his smile dimmed. "Wish I could say I cooked it myself, but Pauline made this. The ranch's chef. She's amazing. I'm sure it'll be fantastic."

Even as Archer moved to stand at the other side of the bar, he asked, "Um, why'd you bring me dinner?" Realizing how rude that sounded, he quickly added, "Not that I'm not grateful. It really does smells wonderful."

"My buddies told me you're overworked and understaffed," Lludd replied bluntly, glancing at him repeatedly while taking several large containers out of the bag. "I also wanted a chance to apologize for scaring you in the barn the other night. I thought you were someone else, but that's no excuse." Lludd shook his head, grimacing. Then he met

Archer's gaze and winked. "Plus, a way to a man's heart is through his stomach, or so I've been told."

Lips parting in shock at that statement, Archer didn't know how to respond.

Lludd didn't seem to need him to. "So." He held up a plastic serving spoon that he must have taken from the canister sitting near the butcher block. "I understand that cooked spaghetti squash has about eight net carbs in it. Do I need to find a measuring cup to be exact? Or is it okay to wing it? Do you count carbs religiously or . . ." His voice trailed off in an obvious fishing attempt.

That was when Archer really looked at the food in the container Lludd indicated. It was not filled with spaghetti noodles. Instead, strands of some kind of yellow vegetable were coiled within.

Spaghetti squash, he'd said. And he asked about carbs.

"H-How'd you know?"

While Archer's food choices sometimes confused his co-workers, he never went out of his way to share his eating habits with them. Instead, he answered questions when asked.

"Oh. Nicholas said you mentioned it when they offered you food last night."

Archer cocked his head. Some of his recollections from the previous evening were a little sketchy. He figured it was due to shock. After all, it wasn't every day that one learned that humans weren't walking the earth alone.

Taking that at face value, Archer nodded. "I don't keep real close track," he admitted. "Under fifty a day is ballpark for me, since I'm already fit and keep so active."

He turned his attention to the meat sauce, and his mouth watered. Not only did chunks of some kind of ground meat float in the red fluid, but so did slices of Italian sausage, mushrooms, black olives, and onions. His nose told him there were seasonings in there, too, but he'd never been a chef and couldn't tell too many apart.

Lludd spooned a dollop of the spaghetti squash into each bowl, then covered it in a healthy amount of meat sauce. "There's plenty more." He indicated the bowls still on the counter. "And hopefully some for your lunch tomorrow." As Lludd held out a fork, knife, and spoon, he commented wryly, "Paranormals eat more than humans, but Pauline gave me plenty to bring."

Taking the silverware absently, Archer could only nod. He wasn't even certain when Lludd had located them and placed them on the counter. Having the gargoyle in his kitchen was just so . . . surreal.

"Shall we sit?" Lludd asked, grabbing his own bowl and silverware and crossing to the table. Before he sat, he muttered, "Oh, I brought some of that scotch you liked. Or would you like water? Or something you have here?"

Lludd stood beside the table with a quizzical expression on his face.

Suddenly, a bit more of that scotch sounded like a damn fine idea.

"Uh, the scotch, please. Thanks, uh, Lludd."

Appearing pleased, Lludd returned to the kitchen while Archer transferred his dinner to the table. "The tumblers are—"

"Spotted them earlier," Lludd assured. "Ice?" He began moving to the refrigerator that had a water and ice dispenser.

"No, thanks."

Lludd brought the bottle and two tumblers to the table. He poured a healthy couple of fingers into each tumbler, then pushed one toward Archer. "So, thank you again for allowing me inside your home," he stated, settling at the table.

Archer thought the man suddenly appeared nervous.

Not a man. Gargoyle. Of course, he's clearly male.

After all, there was no way Archer could miss Lludd's broad shoulders, wide pectorals, and ripped torso. He was all man in all the ways that mattered. Even the loincloth couldn't hide the bulge of his prick.

Oh!

The way to a man's . . . no way!

Apologizing for a misunderstanding. Bringing someone a meal. Making certain said meal was something within a person's chosen dietary guidelines.

Those were all courting gestures.

Archer could hardly process that idea as he began cutting his spaghetti with his knife and fork. After making certain all the noodles were thoroughly coated, he scooped up a small mouthful. He slid it into his mouth and nearly moaned at the flavors bursting across his tongue. Enjoying the taste of the meat mixed with the vegetables and seasonings, Archer took his time swallowing.

When Archer opened his eyes — *when did I close them* — he met Lludd's gaze. He spotted the arousal swimming in the male's odd, pale-yellow gaze. Even his nostrils were flaring a little.

Oh. Damn.

While Archer wanted to chalk it up to having not been laid in so long, he couldn't deny his response to that expression.

Yeah . . . I think Lludd wants me. Do humans actually copulate with gargoyles? Oh, right. Nicholas and Bodb. Of course they do.

"The noises you make while eating . . ." Lludd rumbled, a visible shudder running through his body. "Damn."

"Sorry," Archer forced out. "I-I didn't mean to moan out loud. I" — he felt his cheeks heat, and it wasn't all from embarrassment, but he plowed ahead — "I haven't had Italian in over a year and this . . . so much better than I remember."

Lludd's voice came out husky as he stated, "I'm so very glad."

Clearing his throat, Archer reached for his drink and took a sip of his liquor. The burn of the drink helped ease the lustful cobwebs that had abruptly begun clouding his brain. He didn't know how he could suddenly be thinking of Lludd as a possible sexual partner.

God, I shot the guy last night.

There was a sobering thought.

Archer scooped up another forkful of food and took a bite. As he chewed, he sighed happily. Regardless of the reason, he sure appreciated the food.

"Oh, damn," Lludd muttered, rising from his seat. He crossed to the warming satchel still on the counter and opened a side pocket. From within, he pulled a canister before returning to the table. "I forgot. Do you want parmesan cheese?"

Caught off guard, Archer hesitated. Registering Lludd's expectant expression, he pulled his head out of his ass. He might be tired, but he really needed to be a better host.

As if I've done anything remotely host-like this evening.

Lludd had come in and taken over.

"Um, yeah," Archer murmured, pushing his bowl toward Lludd. "Thank you." Unable to help himself, he asked, "Any idea how many carbs are in the meat sauce?"

"I have a fair idea about net carbs," Lludd began. "I looked it up a little on my phone while waiting for you to get home." His expression turned sheepish as he shook some of the cheese from the shaker into Archer's bowl. "Paranormals really don't think about such things, since our metabolism is so much faster and more efficient than a human's." As Lludd began to shake some cheese onto his own food, he continued as if he hadn't said something a bit rude—maybe he hadn't realized it. "Uh, the meal was for just the two of us, so Pauline doubled it. Two jars of sauce at seven net carbs per six serving jar. Eighty-four there, then maybe another five carbs between the mushrooms and black olives. Seasonings don't have anything. So, let's round it out to about ninety carbs for the batch of meat sauce, since there's no carbs in the meat."

It took a few seconds for Archer to catch up with the math. Then he hummed. "Huh. Not bad. Ninety carbs in twelve servings, so seven-point-five, then add in the squash." He talked out loud just for something to say. "So, around sixteen per serving." Then Archer laughed and looked at his bowl. "Of course, I'm pretty sure I ended up with a double serving, so maybe thirty-two. Still not too bad all things considered."

Then Archer noticed Lludd's expectant gaze. He only had to wonder a second to learn what the male was interested in.

"Is that too much for your dietary needs?" Lludd asked. "I can be more careful next time. I can learn to care for you."

"I-I—" Archer swallowed hard. "Y-You want to care for me?"

Lludd smiled widely as he nodded eagerly.

Confused, Archer cocked his head. "Why? I shot you. I don't even know how you're up and around." As he said the words, he knew how true they were. "Did I not hit you after all?"

"Oh, no, you hit me," Lludd told him. His tone actually sounded impressed, and his next words told him why. "You're a damn fine shot, Archer. I'm honored to call you mine."

"Y-Yours?" Archer narrowed his eyes, more confused than ever by everything happening. "What the hell is that supposed to mean?"

CHAPTER SIX

"Oh, fuck." Lludd heaved a sigh as his shoulders drooped. He used his fork to swirl his spaghetti. He took a bite just to buy time to think. After swallowing, knowing he needed to be honest, he met Archer's gaze. "I got carried away. Your scent." Lludd inhaled deeply, unable to help himself. His prick throbbed behind the fly of the jeans he'd donned for the flight over. "Well, paranormals live for so very long." He cocked his head. "Bodb and Nicholas said you were pretty overwhelmed by everything, and I don't know if they told you about our swift healing or longevity or lack of ability to get human diseases. I know they didn't tell you about mates, so—"

"Whoa, whoa."

Archer held up his free hand, and Lludd fell silent. He watched as his mate took a sip of his drink, then scooped up more food. At least his mate was still eating the food he'd provided. That calmed Lludd's nature.

"You're talking really fast, telling me you're nervous," Archer stated, seeming to read him easily. "So, first, yes. Bodb assured me that you would be fine, then explained about your increased healing. That led to a comment about how it helped you all live longer, but he didn't give specifics." Then Archer popped a bite of food into his mouth and chewed. At the same time, he pointed at Lludd's own bowl.

Taking the unspoken question at face value, Lludd refrained from speaking and ate a couple of bites instead.

After Archer had done the same, he asked, "How long do

paranormals live?"

Lludd took a moment to swallow and think. He tried to take Bodb's words of thinking before speaking to heart. "Well, the paranormals that live on the earthen plane of existence, most of them live upward of five hundred years. Uh, like vampires and shifters. Gargoyles are a little different, maybe because we don't reproduce as swiftly or because we are all male or even because we don't get a human form until after we bond." Lludd snapped his mouth shut, realizing he rambled and that he was overwhelming his mate by the way his eyes had begun to widen. Clearing his throat, he took a chance, reaching over and resting his clawed hand over Archer's wrist. "A gargoyle can live around two millennia. At the moment, I'm just over twelve hundred years old." Then, unable to help himself, Lludd whispered, "I've been waiting for my mate, for you, for so very long, Archer. I-I can't wait to-to finally hold you. Touch you. Give you ultimate pleasure as we twine our life forces and build a life together."

Upon seeing the way Archer's jaw sagged open and his eyes widened, Lludd knew he'd totally jumped the gun. He eased his hold on his mate's wrist. Settling his thumb over his human's pulse point, he rubbed every-so-lightly, massaging.

"W-Wow," Archer whispered huskily. He set down his fork, then used that hand to grab his drink. After knocking the rest back in one swallow, Archer returned it to the table with a clunk. "Th-That was . . . unexpected."

"I apologize for dumping it on you that way," Lludd murmured. "My brother always tells me to think before speaking, and I really thought I was, but" — grimacing, he finished — "yeah, I guess I botched that up. Huh?"

Archer barked a harsh laugh, but he did meet Lludd's gaze. "Never had a guy propose on a first date." Sweeping his free hand between their nearly empty bowls of food, he asked, "This was meant to be a date, right?"

Lludd would deny it to his dying day, but he did feel the heat that rushed to his cheeks. "W-Well, um —" Seeing Archer lift one brow in silent question, he nodded once. "If I could finagle it. Yeah." Lludd pointed at the meal. "A way to woo you. To show you that I'm not some feral beast."

Slowly, Archer looked down at where Lludd continued to massage his wrist. "I admit, when I first saw you, that's what I thought." He rested his free hand on Lludd's hand and began rubbing his fingertips over his knuckles. "Damn, that feels different."

Realizing Archer referred to his leathery hide and had blurted that out without meaning to, Lludd didn't call attention to it. Instead, he fought against the goose bumps that threatened to rise on his mottled, medium-purple-hided arm. If he'd had hair there, it would have been standing on end from the pleasure of Archer's oh-so-innocent touch.

Archer must have shaken himself out of his musings. Stopping his soothing rubbing, he rested his hand over the back of Lludd's. He frowned, nibbled his lips, then swallowed hard enough to cause his Adam's apple to bob.

Lludd saw the rejection coming a mile away.

Unable to hear those words after searching for his mate for so long, Lludd blurted out, "Are you not even going to ask me about mates before you tell me we're not right for each other?"

Archer opened his mouth, then closed it again.

Sighing deeply, Lludd stared at his food. Unable to see that look in his mate's gorgeous green eyes anymore. "I'm sorry, Archer. I wish I could just let you go if you asked me to." He glanced his human's way, but only up to his chin, then back to his food. "Not only do I not want to, but Fate likes to get her way and is pretty manipulative. I hear she sends . . . dreams . . . to the human. Erotic ones. Ones that leave you aching with need." Lludd slowly released Archer and pulled away from him. Resting his palms on either side of his bowl, he forced himself to stare Archer in the eye. "Humans require wooing. I get that." He jerked a nod. "I'll do that for you. Find a way to." Holding out his hand, Lludd wiggled his fingers. "Archer, will you give me your phone so I can have your telephone number?"

To Lludd's surprise, Archer chuckled huskily. "You do like to jump to conclusions. Don't you?"

Returning his hand to the table, Lludd muttered, "Huh?"

Archer smirked. "I was actually going to ask how you can know I'm your mate or how you choose."

Lludd's lips parted as shock filled him. "Oh, damn. I-I'm sorry."

Lifting one hand to silence Lludd, Archer picked up his fork with the other. "So, for the remainder of the meal, I'll ask questions. You'll answer them, and you will not try to guess what I'm thinking." Winking, Archer scooped up his food. "Because you're obviously not very good at it." Then he popped the bite of food into his mouth.

After an instant, Lludd nodded and followed his mate's example. "Uh, you asked how I know you're my mate," Lludd began slowly. "And no, we don't choose. Fate does." Upon seeing Archer's disbelieving expression, he quickly rushed on. "I know it sounds unbelievable, but she really does exist. And before you think the only reason I like you is because Fate says you're my mate, that's not the way it works either." For once, Lludd appreciated his propensity to speak bluntly. "Think of it as . . . she finds two compatible people in a time when they need each other. Even though they would have been attracted to each other, because of circumstances, they might ignore that for one reason or another. Fate gives us that *push*, that increased awareness of each other and arousal and need for each other, to push through our reservations and take a chance on the relationship."

"Huh," Archer murmured, nodding slowly as he used his spoon to scoop up the last of his spaghetti. "Okay." Before popping his spoon into his mouth, Archer asked, "How does this binding our lives together work?" He dipped his gaze down, as if he could look beneath the table, before meeting Lludd's gaze again and asked, "Are we even compatible?" Then Archer's brows furrowed. "Or is this bonding not sexual?"

A feral growl escaped Lludd before he could stop it as arousal surged through his body. Upon seeing Archer's brows shoot up, he did his best to school himself. With the need thrumming through his system—it wasn't easy sitting in his mate's home, his sensitive senses permeated by his human's scent—Lludd shuddered with need.

Archer must have noticed, for his eyes widened. His lips parted and his tongue darted out, wetting his bottom lip. Even his green eyes dilated.

Every instinct Lludd possessed screamed at him to pull Archer onto his lap and claim his mouth.

Evidently, Archer regained his control first. "S-So." He cleared his throat. "Sexual."

"Yes," Lludd confirmed gruffly. "A paranormal bonds for life. No other." Just the idea of Archer with another caused his blood to boil. He grabbed his scotch and downed the last of his own. Then he grabbed the bottle and poured more into his glass before offering to do the same to Archer's. "More?"

Archer shook his head, then nodded. "Thanks."

Lludd poured him a couple of fingers, then placed the decanter on the table. "So, yes. Sexual." Flexing his claws, he told Archer, "I intend to make your body sing."

After taking a small sip of his drink, probably to buy time, Archer met Lludd's gaze once more. "And this issue of our difference in lifespans?"

"Yours will extend to match mine."

Even though Lludd hadn't intended to share all this information until he'd spent more time with Archer, he appreciated that his human was willing to discuss such things. His human even seemed pretty open to the idea. Well, the arousal burning off the human's skin certainly betrayed his interest.

However, Lludd was old enough to know that he couldn't go off that scent alone. He needed verbal cues, too. His mate needed to say the words.

"Damn." Archer pushed his bowl away, then cradled his tumbler between his palms. "Okay, don't think I'm refusing, but can you give me time?"

Lludd felt his chest tighten, but he forced himself to nod. "I figure you need some time to process," he commented softly. "May I still see you?"

Archer hesitated before nodding once. "I think I would like that." After sipping his drink, he pointed at Lludd's bowl and began, "Can I get you—" Whatever he intended to ask was captured by a jaw-cracking yawn.

After a quick glance at the clock on the oven, Lludd felt a niggle of guilt. It was well past ten-thirty, and he'd been told his mate was burning the candle at both ends—or so the saying went.

Lludd quickly rose and gripped Archer's shoulders. Standing that close, he realized he towered over his mate by nearly a foot. He knew if he tugged Archer against him, his human would fit oh-so-perfectly against his bigger body.

Resisting the desire, Lludd ordered, "Finish your drink, then get ready for bed. I'll clean up."

"You don't have to do that," Archer resisted. "I can get the dishes in the morning."

Shaking his head, Lludd dipped and bussed a kiss to Archer's temple. He took a few seconds to revel in the soft flesh under his lips. His mate's scent flooded his senses, doing more to intoxicate him than any alcohol ever could.

Lludd felt the tremble work through the body in his arms, and he barely resisted the urge to reel him in. Tightening his control, he lifted his head and straightened. Giving his mate a rueful smile, he backed away.

"You're going to be trouble, Archer," Lludd rumbled as he started toward the kitchen with the bowls. "Go. I'll see myself out."

"Are you sure?" Archer seemed uncertain.

Smiling tightly, Lludd nodded. "Oh, yeah. If I stay much longer in your home, with your scent permeating my senses, I'm afraid I'll push." He took a step backward. "And I don't want to do that to you. I don't want to be that asshole. I—" After a glance over his shoulder, Lludd forced himself to focus on starting the water and finding the dish soap. "We'll come together in your time, Archer."

Lludd knew he was a little impulsive, so he knew it would be tough, but he could do that for his mate.

Feeling Archer's hand on his arm, Lludd stilled, but he didn't turn.

"By the way, Lludd," Archer murmured softly. "I don't count carbs that stringently, so don't fret about it." His grip tightened before he said, "And yes, I'll give you my phone number. Where's your phone? I'll dial mine."

Praying his hand didn't shake, Lludd dried his hand on a towel. Then he unclipped his phone from the holder attached to the leather straps criss-crossing his body. He handed over the device.

As Lludd watched, Archer tapped at the screen. A few seconds later, a chime sounded in his mate's pocket. He handed it back, and Lludd reclipped it to himself.

"Thank you for dinner and the company, Lludd."

"The pleasure was mine," Lludd whispered back.

Then Archer eased away from him and disappeared down a hallway.

As much as Lludd longed to follow, he did as he said he would. He cleaned their dirty dishes, leaving them in the dish drainer. Then he placed the containers holding their leftovers in his mate's refrigerator.

Being the nosey gargoyle that he was, he poked around at the other items in the fridge, trying to decide on his mate's likes and dislikes.

When the shower turned on, Lludd groaned and palmed his fly. He knew he needed to get out of there before he did something stupid—like strip down and join his mate in the shower. His cock throbbed as he grabbed his hat and slapped it on his head. Then Lludd replaced the stick he'd seen Archer remove from the slider of his sliding glass door, since he couldn't put it in from the outside.

Lludd let himself out the front door, locking the knob before closing it. Pulling his phone from his harness, he quickly saved his mate's info. Finally, he punched out a text to his mate.

Lock the deadbolt on your front door.

Then Lludd sat in a tree and waited until he received confirmation and heard the click of the lock before flying home.

CHAPTER SEVEN

A rcher had to admit that he'd missed Lludd's company the
prior evening. While the gargoyle had texted that he'd
left dinner on the back step, he'd apologized that he wouldn't
be able to join him. As Archer had enjoyed a pair of succulent
pork chops seasoned in some kind of dry rub, as well as a
healthy serving of steamed and buttered cauliflower, he'd
wondered what could be so important.

Then Archer realized how selfish that was.

The male had his own duties to attend to, after all. Due to
the fact that unmated gargoyles slept all day as a stone
statue—something they called roost—their work just happened to take place at night. Lludd was a guard for Elder
Bodb, and since he'd been out from a gunshot wound one
night and spending several hours for dinner the next evening,
he probably had plenty to work to make up for.

"Hey, boss man!" There was a definite note of amusement
in Deputy Geraldo Martinez's voice. "You need to come out
here."

While Archer and Geraldo were friends, they normally
weren't that informal in the workplace. Intrigued, he rose and
headed out of his office. He glanced around and spotted
Geraldo up front near the reception desk.

As Archer approached, he noticed Marinette Rosado's
desk chair was empty, and he glanced at his watch.

Huh. Twelve-twenty already. Where had the morning gone?

That meant, with their receptionist on lunch, Geraldo was
filling in. The poor man had agreed to do a double shift when

Deputy Margo Whitehouse had called in. She'd come down with the cold that was sweeping through their ranks and had sounded horrible.

"What is it, Geraldo?" he asked just before he spotted the delivery man on the other side of the desk.

Geraldo's big, broad body had been blocking the skinny kid's frame . . . and the gift basket sitting on the desk. His deputy wasn't your typical Hispanic. While he had the traditional bronzed skin and features, his body frame had ended up being a throwback to his large, African grandfather's. Geraldo stood six-foot-three and was built like a linebacker but moved with the grace of a wide receiver.

"You have a delivery, Sheriff," Geraldo told him with a rakish grin. "And your signature is required."

"Okay."

Archer stopped at the desk and took the electronic pad from the guy who was staring at Geraldo appreciatively . . . and none-too-subtly. For his deputy's part, he didn't seem to notice. After signing, Archer handed the pad back and turned his attention to the delivery.

The basket was of medium size, maybe a foot in diameter. It was wrapped in a translucent pale-green cellophane with a dark-green bow holding it together at the top. He noticed a couple of boxes and packages tucked inside, but he couldn't make out the words on them.

Intrigued, Archer picked it up and took it back to his office. When he set it on the desk, he noticed Geraldo had followed, a shit-eating grin on his lips. Lifting one brow, Archer smirked at his deputy.

Geraldo scoffed and waved his hand at the package. "Come on, man. Don't leave me hangin'," he whined. "I didn't even know you were seein' somebody. Who's it from?"

Archer could guess, but he decided to needle his friend a little. "How do you know it's from someone I'm seeing?" He crossed his arms over his chest. "Maybe it's from someone grateful for our services."

Rolling his eyes, Geraldo shook his head. "If that were the case, anyone here could have signed for it." He pointed at Archer. "This was sent specifically to you."

Okay. He's got me there.

Smirking, Archer returned his focus to the package. He was damn curious. Grabbing the end of the bow, he carefully opened it. After removing the ribbon, he discovered a twist tie hidden discreetly beneath it, which had really been holding it closed. Archer took that off, too.

Archer peeled the layers of cellophane back, revealing the contents. He spotted a package of mini cinnamon rolls and pulled them out with curiosity. The label claimed they were grain-free and paleo-friendly. Unable to help himself, he checked the ingredients.

"Huh. Almond flour." Then Archer looked at the carb count. "Net ten for two. Not bad for a treat, assuming they're any good."

"Oh, wow. All this stuff is grain-free treats," Geraldo commented. He'd moved closer and was poking through the contents. "Dark-chocolate-covered pecans, almond flour blueberry and chocolate, chocolate-chip muffins, cassava flour crackers and tortilla chips, salsa, salami, goat cheese." Geraldo's voice was filled with wonder. "How the hell did your lady fit all this in here?"

Putting the package down, Archer smacked at Geraldo's hand where he was rifling through everything. "Hey, that's mine. Ever think I woulda wanted to discover everything myself?"

In truth, Archer was feeling a little overwhelmed. When he'd told Lludd that he didn't really count his carbs too closely, he said it to reassure the concerned male. He'd noticed the tension in Lludd's body when he'd begun spouting off statistics about the meal. Obviously, the gargoyle had wanted to set Archer's mind at ease.

It had been really thoughtful.

This, however, *this* was even more thoughtful. He'd gone out of his way to track down a plethora of treats that still fit within his dietary plans. Well, as long as he was careful about how much he ate at one time.

Completely ignoring him, Geraldo reached back into the basket. "Hey, there's a note."

Before Geraldo could open it, Archer snagged it away from him. "Hands off," he growled, which only earned him a cackle from his deputy.

Opening it, Archer read —

My dearest mate,

Thank you so much for giving me the opportunity to spend Tuesday evening with you. I pray to the gods that we'll have many such an evening together and more. Until that time, know that you're in my thoughts.

While I know some of these treats are a bit higher in carbs than you normally indulge in, I hope as you savor each bite, you are reminded that I feel the same of each moment I get to spend with you.

Thinking of you, L

"Holy shit, she's clearly smitten and a bit of a poet."

Archer snapped his head up. He'd been so focused on Lludd's words that he hadn't noticed Geraldo sidle close to read over his shoulder. It was on the tip of his tongue to correct the pronoun, but Archer hesitated.

Then Archer thought of how thoughtful it was of Lludd to use his initial, just in case he wasn't out. Except, technically, he *wasn't* out, at least not to anyone in his department. It just hadn't come up. Archer had never had anyone attempting to claim him as his own before.

Still, unwilling to lie, even by omission, Archer decided with only Geraldo in the office, it was a good time to test the waters. If his closest friend on the force was going to have an issue with it, he needed to know as soon as possible. After all, Archer wasn't going to deny Lludd once they got together.

And when the fuck did I decide we'd get together?

As soon as Archer had the thought, he knew the answer. Hell, even if he wasn't experiencing the most erotic wet dreams of his life, Lludd's thoughtfulness of his eating habits showed he cared. The gargoyle probably had to go to a lot of work to put the gift basket together. Seeing as Lludd couldn't go to the city, which was probably where most of the stuff had to be picked up, he would have needed to beg assistance from someone.

"Actually, wrong pronoun, Geraldo," Archer stated, taking a step sideways to place the desk between them. At the same time, he slid the basket closer to him and picked up the blueberry muffin. "L stands for Lludd."

Geraldo's eyebrows shot up. His dark, nearly black eyes rounded. Then a wide grin split his lips.

"Oh, hey, I didn't know you were like me." Geraldo waggled his brows. "You should have told me you were bisexual. We coulda gone bar hoppin' together sometime."

It suddenly hit Archer that he'd been holding himself back. He could have had a much closer relationship with Geraldo if he'd been honest with his friend. Realizing it wasn't too late, he shrugged.

"I lean more toward the gay side of that, Geraldo," Archer admitted to him with a smirk. "Never found a woman who interested me . . . so maybe just gay."

Geraldo chuckled as he nodded. "All right, man." He lifted his fist, and Archer bumped it. "So, gonna share? How long you been with Lludd? When do I get to meet him?"

Laughing, Archer reached in and grabbed the double chocolate chip muffin and tossed it to him. "Cut off a bite for me, but you can have the rest." He knew what a chocolate fiend the man was.

His expression lighting up, Geraldo nodded. "Sweet."

"And it's new, so we're still feeling our way," Archer told him, opening his own muffin package. "Give me a little more time before immersing him in the politics of my life."

"True that." Geraldo tore off a small chunk of his muffin and placed it back in his package. He slid that across the desk toward Archer. "So, think Mayor We-Know-Is-Dirty is going to try to ask for a recall after you come out?"

Archer dropped the small chunk he'd just torn off his muffin onto his wrapper, more from surprise than a planned movement. "I hadn't thought of that," he admitted as he pushed the bit of muffin toward Geraldo so he could try that flavor, too. "You think Darcy learned his bigoted attitude from Sheldon?"

Then Archer took a bite of the blueberry muffin. As the smooth flavor of blueberry and sweetness flowed across his tongue, he hummed appreciatively. He couldn't remember the last time he'd indulged in such a thing, and for Lludd to locate a grain-free option—decadent.

"Oh, damn," Geraldo mumbled around his mouthful. "That's damn good." He swallowed as he picked up the blueberry hunk. "I just might convert. Why'd you switch, anyway?" Geraldo flicked a finger toward Archer's body. "You've always looked fit and trim." Then, before Archer could come up with an answer, he added, "And you know the old saying, the apple doesn't fall far from the tree," before popping the blueberry bit into his mouth.

Geraldo hummed again.

Archer ate the chocolate bite as he mused over Geraldo's comment. After he'd swallowed, he stated, "If that comes up, we'll cross that bridge, but we won't borrow trouble." Narrowing his eyes, he added, "Besides, there are some very powerful gay men and women in this community that could really screw up the mayor's attempt at re-election next year if the local gay sheriff was screwed with."

Cocking his head, Geraldo split his lips into a shit-eating grin. "Yeah, there are." Then he held up a finger and headed out of the office, continuing to scarf his muffin.

As Archer waited for his deputy to return, he savored his own muffin. He hadn't recognized the brand, but he sure enjoyed it. He wondered if he could buy them online, since he couldn't imagine making it into the city to go to a specialty or large chain store any time soon.

Archer had just finished his muffin and was using a napkin to clean his fingers when Geraldo returned.

"We had a couple of new resumes come in this morning." Geraldo placed a couple of folders on his desk. "They look far more promising than any of the others."

"Really?" Archer grinned, relieved that his father had come through for him, although he was surprised he hadn't called to give him a heads up. "That's excellent news."

Archer threw away his garbage and pulled the first one toward him. "You already read through these, then?" he asked needlessly as he flipped the top one open.

"Yep."

"Okay." Archer met Geraldo's gaze. "After I read through them, I'll talk to you about your thoughts."

Geraldo gave him a thumbs up and headed away, calling, "Thanks for the muffin."

Archer focused on the first file—Marco Sanchez. It appeared pretty straightforward. He worked in a department out of Dallas and had several recommendations in his file for excellent work and acting calm under pressure. In his resume, Marco indicated that he was looking for something with a slightly slower pace with the opportunity to return to his ranching roots.

While Marco sounded about perfect, Archer knew he

would need to talk to the man's superior officers before calling the man for an interview.

Opening the second folder, Archer paused over the name—Sandro Virche. Then he looked at the picture. He immediately saw the resemblance. The man looked damn similar to Spieron.

Is this man a vampire?

Even as Archer looked through the file at Sandro's accolades and commendations, he wondered if they were true. He was supposedly from Houston, but was that true? His hand hovered over the phone, but he wasn't certain who he wanted to call—Sandro's chief or Bodb.

Was the gargoyle trying to get a paranormal into his department? If so, why?

Lowering his hand, Archer realized he couldn't ask shit like that over the phone, either.

Archer rose, closing the file. He placed the one for Marco in the top drawer, then picked up the one for Sandro. After tucking the file into his satchel, he slung the strap over his shoulder.

Closing his office door behind him, Archer headed across the floor, seeing Marinette had returned from lunch. He caught Geraldo's eye and told him, "I need to run out and see about that tip we got on the Lindson ranch again. I'll be back in a bit."

Although there was a questioning gleam in Geraldo's eyes, the big man didn't voice it. He just dipped his head in a nod and said, "I'll hold down the fort."

"Thanks." As Archer passed Marinette, he requested, "Please forward anything important to my cell."

"Will do, Sheriff," Marinette replied brightly. The woman always wore a smile, and it never failed to brighten Archer's day.

Archer strode out of the precinct and down the front walk. He'd just reached the bottom of the steps when he spotted someone he didn't want to see. Groaning under his breath, he realized he'd forgotten all about Darcy's interview.

"Hey, Archer," Darcy called disrespectfully, a fake grin and cold gleam in his blue eyes. "Meeting me out front?"

After a quick glance at the time on his phone, Archer realized Darcy was a good fifteen minutes early. "No, Deputy Loreman, I was heading to get coffee before our interview. Also, please remember to call me Sheriff Montgomery."

Darcy almost rolled his eyes. Archer could see him stop himself just in time.

Instead, Darcy glanced around and shrugged. "Sorry. No one's around, and we're not in the office."

Well, that was the most insincere apology I've ever heard.

"That may very well be, but we are both in uniform," Archer reminded him. "Please use ranks unless we're both off the clock."

As if I'd ever want to hang out with him in my spare time.

"Okay, Sheriff Montgomery," Darcy replied with a hint of annoyance in his voice.

"Thank you," Archer replied. "Now then. I'm in need of some coffee other than the station swill. Can I bring you a cup?"

Darcy nodded. "Yeah, thanks. A cappuccino would be great."

"See you in ten, Deputy Loreman," Archer told him, turning away.

So much for heading out to the ranch.

Pulling out his phone, Archer sent Geraldo a quick text.

Ran into Darcy outside the office. Forgot about his interview. Please lock my office. Have him wait in the bullpen.

Then Archer strode down the street to pick up a good cup of coffee, giving him a moment to get his head in the right mindset to deal with Darcy.

Archer's phone pinged as he entered the coffee house two blocks from the office.

Done. And boy is he pissed.

That was followed up by laughing smileys with tears in its eyes.

Smirking, Archer ordered their coffees.

CHAPTER EIGHT

When Lludd woke from roost, he immediately sensed he wasn't alone. He lifted his head from his bowed position and spotted Bodb in his true form, sitting cross-legged on one of the sleeping pallets Nicholas had insisted be put in the barn loft. The unmated gargoyles found it amusing, since they were stone during the day and couldn't feel the comfort, but the thought was a nice one.

"Brother," Lludd greeted as he rose to his feet and stretched his arms over his head. He spread his wings and arched his back, getting the blood flowing through his body. "What's up?"

Lludd noticed Biscane, the only other unmated gargoyle in their small clutch-like group, rising and doing the same as him, although he eyed Bodb curiously.

Bodb smiled at them both. "After you get cleaned up, plan on staying at the ranch house for a meeting. Something has come up." He glanced between them. "Sindrid will be on patrol duty with you this evening, Biscane. Sorry."

Biscane nodded. "No problem, Elder." He winked at Lludd. "Figured since Lludd found his mate his schedule would get a little wonky."

After a smile of thanks, Bodb met Lludd's gaze again.

"My mate? Sounds ominous," Lludd stated, frowning. "What's up?" Then he noticed a scent in the air, although faint. "Archer was here. You touched him."

"Shook hands, yes," Bodb confirmed. "And he's still here, waiting for you." His brother rose and leaped onto the stack of hay that separated their discreet roosting area from the rest of the hayloft. "Hurry up. Your mate needs you."

Lludd and Biscane exchanged glances, then followed Bodb out of the loft. As much as Lludd wished he could head straight to the house, he knew he should freshen up first. Otherwise, he'd bear the scents of his sweat from the prior day as well as the smells from the barn he'd roosted in—horse, manure, leather, and hay.

Jumping from the open loft door, Lludd spread his wings and flew swiftly to the bunkhouse. He and Biscane separated in the hallway, each choosing a bathroom. As they were both showering at the same time, Lludd appreciated the upgraded facilities Nicholas and Bodb had installed when they renovated the bunkhouse as they moved more paranormals onto the ranch.

Seeing as many of them had lived long enough to know what it was like not to have indoor plumbing, paranormals relished their little luxuries.

After cleaning up in record time, Lludd rushed from the bunkhouse and flew across the yard to the main house's back door. He strode inside, his senses immediately assaulted by the smell of food. His stomach rumbled, but he ignored it in favor of tracking down his mate.

To Lludd's pleasure, he found Archer in the dining room. The man was sipping a beer and conversing with Maggie. They seemed to be deep in discussion about magick, which, from his expression, Archer must have found fascinating.

As soon as they noticed Lludd, Archer smiled, albeit hesitantly.

Just as Lludd opened his mouth to greet Archer, Maggie scowled at him. "If you call me fat again, I'll cast a spell on you so you can't get it up for a month."

Lludd grimaced as he hunched his shoulders, taking in Archer's shocked expression. He'd forgotten he hadn't seen the pregnant woman since his unthinking comment a few days before. Trying to do damage control, Lludd lifted his hands in placation as he racked his brain for the right thing to say.

"I'm sorry, Maggie," Lludd began, slowly moving toward the table. He watched as the woman continued to eye him distrustfully. "I didn't mean to call you fat. Pregnant women aren't fat. They're pregnant." As Maggie arched one brow, Lludd stopped next to the table. "It's been a long time since I've been around someone suffering from pregnancy hormones, and I forgot how it can seem . . . how it affects how something can be construed. I—"

"You think pregnancy hormones change your words?" Maggie shrieked, rising from the table. "How else would you interpret that you"—she lifted her fingers in air quotes—"yes, I can see your waistline increasing."

Lludd knew the conversation was once again getting out of control, but he didn't know how to fix it. He still didn't understand what he'd said that was so wrong. All he'd done was answer Maggie's question honestly.

"Well, I can . . . because you're pregnant," Lludd pointed out. "Why would that surprise you? It's expected. You glow with—"

"And now I'm a fat sweaty mess?" Maggie snarled.

"No!" Lludd glanced around uneasily, but while he saw several people watching—some with wide eyes and some with amusement—no one looked like they were going to step in. Lludd thrust his fingers through his hair and growled. "Why do you take everything I say wrong, damn it. I didn't say anything about sweat or being messy. I said—"

Suddenly, Lludd felt a hand slap over his mouth. Another hand rested on his lower back, causing tingles to erupt over his skin. He turned his attention to the left and saw Archer standing beside him.

Archer peered at Maggie with a beseeching smile. "Please don't curse him with erectile dysfunction for a month, Maggie. I beg of you. I don't think I could go that long without sex." Then he turned to Lludd and lifted both brows. "And I'm sure when Lludd said you glowed it was because you're the picture of gorgeous, pregnant health." After Lludd nodded, Archer turned his attention back to Maggie. "It has nothing to do with sweat, and no one said anything about being a mess. Really, sweetheart. You're beautiful."

Maggie nibbled her bottom lip, twisting a strand of her brown hair around her forefingers.

"Maggie, baby, what's wrong?" Sandra asked, rushing into the room. "I heard you —" The lithe blond snapped her mouth shut as she skidded to a halt next to Maggie. As she wrapped her arms around her lover, Sandra rolled her eyes. "Really, Lludd? Again? When will you learn to just keep your mouth shut?"

Just as Sandra finished speaking, Maggie burst into tears. She wrapped her arms around Sandra's waist and sagged into her embrace. Burying her face against Sandra's neck, she hiccupped, appearing to try to control herself.

"Seriously, Lludd?" Sandra snarled. "What the hell did you say?"

Lludd opened his mouth, but Archer's fingers over his lips pressed harder, staying his urge to talk. Instead, the desire to lick his human's flesh swept through him. He wanted to taste his mate and enjoy his exquisite flavor.

"It's all my fault."

Maggie's wailing pulled Lludd away from his lustful thoughts.

"I t-took everything o-out of context," Maggie stuttered out around her tears. "H-He didn't c-call me f-fat. Said I-I'm g-gorgeous."

Lludd wasn't certain if that was totally accurate, either, but he knew better than to say anything. Sure, he was blunt and straightforward, but he wasn't stupid.

Sandra turned a surprised look Lludd's way, her brows high on her forehead. "Is that true?"

Archer finally lowered his hand, and Lludd felt a bit of disappointment at not getting the chance to taste him.

Later.

"Uh, not in so many words," Lludd murmured softly, seeing Archer's encouraging expression out of the corner of his eye. Taking his cue from his mate, he added, "But, yeah. I meant Maggie beginning to show her pregnancy makes her appear even more stunning than ever."

Sandra smiled, even though she didn't seem completely convinced.

Fortunately, Maggie lifted her head, revealing her tear-stained face and watery smile. "Thanks," she whispered. Then Maggie focused on Sandra. "Can I have some tea in our room?"

Nodding, Sandra pecked a kiss to Maggie's wet lips. "Of course. I'll take you up and get you situated, then come down and get your favorite mint tea."

"Thank you," Maggie whispered.

Then both women headed upstairs.

As the activity continued around the room, Lludd heaved a relieved sigh. "Thank you," he murmured heartfeltly as he focused on Archer. Gripping his human's hand, he squeezed appreciatively. "You have no idea how much I appreciate your intervention."

Archer smiled up at him. "Happy to help, Lludd." Amusement gleamed in his green eyes. "You do have a penchant for bluntly speaking your mind."

Lludd nodded solemnly. "I do."

"I like it."

Eyes wide with shock, Lludd gaped. "You do?"

"I do," Archer confirmed. "It means I'll always know

where I stand with you." Then he waggled his brows. "Although, I may have to ask you to refrain from speaking to the mayor sometimes, because pissing him off could cause problems with my job." His mirth faded, and Archer peered up at him earnestly. "He's going to cause trouble enough as it is once he realizes I have a man as a partner."

"Partner?" Lludd's pulse spiked in his veins. "A-Are you saying, um—" He struggled to speak the words, for fear he was misunderstanding.

Archer nodded once. "If you're still willing after we talk about what's going on in the community." He grimaced. "We may face some persecution."

Scoffing, Lludd grinned widely. "That's nothing new. There's persecution in one form or another everywhere."

"Lludd," Bodb cut in. "Grab food and drink and join us in the family room." He grinned and winked. "And congrats on finding a mate who can interpret your blunt ramblings for you."

While Archer chuckled, Lludd rolled his eyes. He did release his mate to head over and follow his brother's order, though. After loading up a tray with a variety of foods, Lludd turned his attention to Archer, who stood waiting nearby.

"Can I get you anything?"

Archer stared at his tray and smirked.

Lludd knew what he saw. A large sausage, egg, and cheese breakfast burrito had been wrapped in waxed paper to hold it together . . . or to make it easier to be held. There were three slices of three-meat, extra-cheese pizza. The bacon double cheeseburger oozed sautéed mushrooms and onions. Lludd had skipped the chips in favor of a cheesy, hash brown casserole with small, diced ham cubes in it. He'd also added a couple of pieces of cinnamon toast, since cinnamon was a natural contraceptive to gargoyle sperm.

Right. Gotta remember to explain how gargoyles can get male mates pregnant. Later, though.

69

Shrugging and smiling, Lludd reminded his mate, "Para-normals have larger than normal appetites. Remember?"

Chuckling, Archer told him, "If you eat all that, I will never forget again."

Lludd didn't bother to comment. He certainly didn't tell him that he intended to come back for seconds. Instead, he repeated his question.

"Is there anything I can get you?"

"Oh, right." Archer nodded. "A cup of black tea would be great." His eyes narrowed as he lowered his voice to a rumble. "Assuming you still want to be with me, even with the problems I may be facing, I want to be sober and alert for what we may get up to tonight."

Groaning softly, Lludd lowered his hand to his groin. "My handsome mate." He narrowed his eyes. "There is nothing you could ever tell me that would make me walk away from you." Seeing the doubt in Archer's eyes, Lludd stated, "You are my mate. The other half of my soul."

While Archer nodded, his scent betrayed that he was still unconvinced.

That was fine. Lludd knew time was on his side to prove himself. Placing his platter on the counter, he first made a cup of Earl Grey tea for Archer and handed it off to him, then poured himself a cup of coffee. After adding a dash of hazel-nut creamer, Lludd placed his mug on the tray.

"No food?" Lludd asked, pausing.

Archer shook his head. "No, thank you. I'm not hungry." He dunked his teabag a couple of times as he added, "Those pork chops were spectacular, by the way. Thank you."

Lludd beamed, so pleased his mate had appreciated the food he'd asked Pauline to make. "So glad you liked it. It's one of my favorites." Picking up the tray with one hand, he rested his other on the small of Archer's back. "Let's go find a seat and relax."

Then Lludd guided his mate into the family room. It felt so very domestic, heading in to eat and talk with family, that his heart nearly burst with pride. He'd found his mate, and he was joining his family and friends for a meal.

Of course, Lludd wished they were bonded, but he knew they would get there.

Lludd entered the room and glanced around. The space was pretty full, but they'd left a love seat open to them. Someone had even placed a TV tray next to it for Lludd's tray.

After guiding Archer to the sofa, Lludd placed the tray down and settled next to him. He picked up a couple of packets of spicy picante sauce and opened them, then grabbed his burrito and unwrapped the top half. After taking a big bite, Lludd glanced around the space.

Noticing the only gargoyles missing were Biscane and Sindred, who were on night duty, Lludd took in who else was in attendance. Bodb and Nicholas were there, of course, as were Spieron and Albert. Virgil and Shaw were also there as well as ranch foreman, Stanley Redfeather.

Not surprisingly, Maggie and Sandra were not there, since they'd headed upstairs so Maggie could rest.

"So," Bodb began, focusing on Lludd. "Archer came out this evening asking about Sandro Virche."

Lludd swallowed. "Is that Spieron's brother?"

Spieron nodded. "Younger. He stayed in a coven I was in decades ago when I was run out for hitting on a donor the second favored." He shrugged. "Oops. Anyway, that coven has gone through some growing pains, and he no longer respects those in charge." Smiling with pleasure, Spieron told him, "He reached out to me to see where I was and ask if my coven would consider taking him in." The vampire grinned widely. "Imagine Sandro's surprise when I told him where I was and who I was with, but I assured him he would still be welcome."

Bodb chuckled. "That was when I recalled hearing that Archer's department is looking for a few people, so I asked around and found a gargoyle tech guru who could give him the background of a kickass deputy." Smirking, Bodb focused on Lludd. "Your mate recognized his name and questioned me about him."

Swallowing his food, Lludd beamed at Archer, already knowing his mate was brilliant. He wasn't a sheriff for nothing, after all.

"I admitted what I'd done, and Archer agreed to hire him." Bodb shrugged. "I don't know who the other guy is, uh, Marco, but then Archer received a text from his father with a heads up on him so."

Lludd didn't know who Marco was either, but he nodded as if following along.

"Unfortunately, that puts Archer in the precarious position of turning down the transfer of the mayor's son to his department." Bodb leveled a serious look Lludd's way. "Between the waves that will create and the fact that Archer is about to announce he has a male partner, he's going to need your support."

Cocking his head, Lludd narrowed his eyes. Then he turned to Archer and stated solemnly. "I suck at politics, but I'll stand by your side until the end of time, my mate."

Archer peered at him with a warm and understanding smile. "I figured that out, and that's okay." Reaching over, he squeezed Lludd's thigh. "I don't care as long as you're by my side."

"It's settled then," Nicholas stated with a clap of his hands. "Lludd, to stand by Archer's side, you need your human form, which means you need to bond." He pointed upstairs. "Third door on the left is a guest suite. Take your food upstairs. Finish eating"—Nicholas waggled his brows—"because you're going to need your strength, and explain bonding to Archer."

CHAPTER NINE

A rcher stared around the room with interest. His gaze fell on the mattress, which appeared soft and comfortable. While the furniture looked a little older with scuffs here and there on the hardwood oak frames, they were in good repair. *Sturdy.*

"Okay," Lludd began, urging Archer toward the front sitting room space. He placed his tray on the coffee table, then pulled Archer down beside him. After wrapping an arm around his shoulders, Lludd peered down at him. "Please know, no matter what Nicholas said earlier, if you're not ready for bonding, we'll wait for however long you want."

While appreciating Lludd's assurances, Archer couldn't deny the arousal thrumming through his body. He fought his desire to glance behind him at the bed beyond. Instead, he held the gargoyle's yellow-eyed gaze.

"I know for certain that I want you by my side, Lludd," Archer admitted even while doing his best not to second guess himself. "God, it's fast."

So damn fast.

Lludd smiled knowingly. "Paranormals do things fast." He tapped his nose before picking up his cheeseburger. "We know our mates by scent, and then we do our best to do whatever is necessary to earn their trust, their heart, and build a life with them." Then Lludd took a big bite.

Smiling upon the hum of appreciation the gargoyle emitted, Archer watched him eat with relish. Chuckling softly, he murmured, "You weren't wrong about how much paranormals can put away."

Archer had been pretty surprised at how few bites it had taken Lludd to put away the breakfast burrito. The gargoyle had even used both packets of hot sauce. Even when Lludd had sniffled a little, he'd still poured more of the hot sauce on there. In four bites, he'd devoured the cinnamon toast. Hell, the gargoyle had even managed to eat one of his pieces of pizza during their short meeting.

After taking a sip of his tea, Archer asked, "So, do you want to tell me how we bond?"

Lludd had just taken another big bite of his burger, but he froze. After a few chews, he swallowed . . . hard. He coughed a couple of times, and Archer leaned over and patted him on his back.

Finally, Lludd rasped, "Sex and blood."

Archer pulled back a little. "Blood?"

Wincing, Lludd put his half-eaten burger on the plate. "Sorry." He wiped his fingers as he explained. "Um, I spill my seed in you." His eyes turned heated, and his expression became feral as his focus slid to Archer's neck. "Then" — Lludd reached out and touched the thick flesh where Archer's neck met his shoulder — "I bite you here, giving you a claiming scar." His focus slid to Archer's eyes, his gaze full of promise. "You will come from it. I bet you'll ask me to bite you often."

Disbelief mixed with hope coursed through Archer. "Really?"

"Mmm-hmm," Lludd assured with a wink. Picking up his burger, before he took another big bite, he added, "Then you can either choose to bite me, too, or I can cut into my flesh somewhere for you to drink from. Most use their wrists."

Archer again found his eyes widening. "You would slice your wrist for me?"

That sounded dangerous.

Lludd swallowed as he winked at Archer. "Not slicing my wrist like you must be thinking." Archer's surprise must have shone on his face, for Lludd continued, "Just deep enough for blood to well up for you to drink. Plus, as a paranormal, I have increased healing, so the mark will be gone in no time."

Nodding slowly, Archer process all that. "So you spill your seed in me, and we exchange blood. Okay." Good thing he was a bottom.

As Archer sipped his tea, he looked over at Lludd, who was still powering through his food. The burger was gone, and he was working his way through a second piece of pizza.

Suddenly, Lludd paused and wiped his hands and face on anther napkin. His deep gray eye ridges, which Archer equated to a gargoyles' eyebrows, were furrowed as he focused on him. He reached over and placed his hand on Archer's thigh.

"I'm sorry. I left off the explanation." Lludd licked his lips as he swept a gaze full of a different kind of hunger over Archer's frame. "You will need to spill your seed in me, too."

Archer sucked in a shocked gasp. "Y-You bottom?"

He looked him over again.

With the gargoyle's massive medium-purple frame and matching dark-gray wings, claws, and hair, Archer never would have guessed. The male was masculine perfection personified—well, as long as someone overlooked the obvious differences between humans and gargoyles.

Hell, maybe that makes him even more attractive to me. He could manhandle me so easily.

Archer's body heated at his thoughts. His blood flowed south, and he swallowed hard. He drank the last of his tea to get a little moisture into his throat.

"For you, my mate." Lludd's rumbly voice drew Archer out of his thoughts. "I will definitely bottom as often as you wish."

Reading between the lines, Archer murmured, "But you'd

rather top, wouldn't you?" When Lludd hesitated to respond, he gave his soon-to-be lover a heated smile. "That's good, because I love feeling a hard body pinning me to the mattress. I'll wrap my legs around your strong waist and rock into each thrust of your hard cock."

As Archer spoke, he peered at Lludd's lap, gratified to see the big bulge pushing against the fabric of his loincloth.

Humming, Archer dared to reach over and cup the length encased in fabric. He groaned upon feeling the thick erection within, imagining the spear splitting him wide open. Pressing and rubbing, he massaged the hidden length.

A low growl drew Archer's attention to Lludd's face. He spotted the heated gleam causing his yellow eyes to nearly glow. Noticing the way Lludd clenched his clawed fists on the outside of his thighs, and how he stared at his groin, watching Archer fondle him, a sensation of power coursed through him.

Somehow, Archer knew that Lludd would allow him to do anything — to and with him.

Ready to put some of his dreams into action, Archer removed his hand. He grinned upon hearing Lludd's moan of dismay. With a wink, he rose to his feet.

"You know, there's a perfectly good bed back here," Archer pointed out, setting down the mug he'd been holding in his other hand. Then he began sauntering around the sofa. "Feel free to finish up." Archer flicked his fingers toward the half-eaten hashbrowns and the last piece of pizza still on Lludd's plate. "I'll just lie down and relax while I wait."

Between one step and the next, Lludd was on him.

Archer felt Lludd's thick arms wrap around his waist. In the next instant, he was flying through the air. Bouncing on his stomach, Archer sprawled on the mattress, his cock throbbing at Lludd's display of strength.

Holy shit!

While Archer had been man-handled before, he'd never

been tossed by a lover.

Hot damn. Hell yeah!

Grinning, Archer peered over his shoulder, pleased to see the feral expression etched across Lludd's features as he stared down at him on the mattress. His body practically vibrated with his obvious need. The loincloth sported a wet spot, accentuating the wide flair of his crown.

"Oh?" Archer teased, rolling onto his back. "Gonna join me after all?" He slid his arms behind his head. "Need a nap?"

Lludd pinned his gaze on Archer's even as he reached for his booted foot. "You will not be napping," he warned, gripping it and pulling the boot and sock from him. "Not for a long, long time." Then Lludd removed his other boot and sock. Resting one knee on the bed, he drew closer. "I've waited so long for this."

When Lludd's clawed hands hovered over Archer's groin, he sucked in a trembling breath. His stomach muscles quivered in anticipation. Even his cock twitched behind his fly.

Except, Lludd hesitated. "Tell me this is what you want," he whispered huskily, his tone tortured. His yellow eyes had gone from hungry to concerned. "Tell me you're okay with me touching you."

Archer realized Lludd had mistaken his body's shaking for trepidation. "Lludd," he purred, reaching up and threading his fingers through the gargoyle's flowing gray hair. "I want this. Can't you smell how much I want you?"

He knew Lludd could.

Lludd nodded once, holding his gaze. "Just because your scent screams *want, want, want,* it doesn't mean that's what a human's mind is saying."

Hearing Lludd's softly spoken words, Archer realized there had to be a story there. Later, he intended to find out what. Right then, he needed to reassure his gargoyle.

Tugging lightly on Lludd's hair, Archer urged the gargoyle

to lever over him. "Do gargoyles kiss, Lludd?" he asked curiously, eyeing the male's sharp canines as he recalled the soft nuzzling pecks Lludd had placed on his temple a couple of nights before.

"We do," Lludd whispered huskily, his focus sweeping over Archer's face.

"Good to know." Archer smiled. "So kiss me."

Lludd let out a noise that sounded like a mix between a whine and a moan. Then he slid his clawed hand into Archer's hair and cradled his head. After an instant more peering into his eyes, Lludd lowered his head and sealed his mouth to Archer's.

With an expert lick and nip, Lludd urged Archer's lips to part. He thrust in his tongue. The gargoyle swirled his appendage around Archer's own, teasing and licking around his mouth.

Archer slid his hands from Lludd's hair to his shoulders. Clinging to the massive expanse of muscles, he opened wide and reveled in the pleasure of being ravished by the gargoyle above him. He tried to keep up, but never in all his years had a lover consumed him so fully. Spots flashed before Archer's eyes, and he feared his dick would explode just from the kiss, without even a touch.

Finally, Lludd broke the kiss, and Archer sucked in a much-needed lungful of air. He realized the spots were caused by a lack of oxygen as he gasped in another breath. After managing to get his breathing sort of under control, Archer grinned up at Lludd.

"Damn," Archer rasped roughly. "Yeah. Yeah, you can kiss."

Lludd chuckled huskily, his expression warm, arousal still simmering within their depths.

"And just so we're clear, Lludd." After seeing the question in his gargoyle's eyes, Archer stated, "I want you. I want to feel your claws on my skin, to feel your tongue on my body, and your erection buried deep inside me." Upon seeing Lludd's lips part in shock and hearing his sharply inhaled gasp, Archer pushed a little bit harder. "I want it so badly, I can taste it. You gonna claim me, my mate?"

A low rumbling growl erupted from the male levered over Archer. Lludd's smile grew, revealing sharp teeth. Massaging Archer's neck, keeping his weight on his other hand, he swept his gaze down Archer's body, then up just as slowly, Lludd finally met his gaze once more.

"I hope you're not partial to those clothes."

Before Archer could take meaning of Lludd's words, he felt the gargoyle shift the hand at his neck. In the next instant, the sound of fabric rending filled the space. Cool air hit the heated flesh of his shoulder as Lludd tore his shirt off his body.

"Damn," Archer whispered, amazed and turned on beyond anything he'd felt before.

Lludd froze, his gaze snapping to Archer's.

Archer saw the questions in Lludd's eyes and gave him a lascivious smile. "I'm not too fond of these jeans, either," he stated with a wink.

A wide smile curved Lludd's lips as he dipped his head. He lowered his head and nuzzled the space where Archer's neck met his shoulder. When Archer tipped his head, offering more room, his gargoyle growled low in his throat.

"Yessss," Lludd hissed.

At the same time, Lludd skimmed the claws of his hand down along Archer's ribs. He teased along his skin, causing goose bumps to rise on his flesh. Then his claws curled into the top of his jeans.

Archer sucked in his gut, giving him more room. At the same time, he moaned and shifted restlessly on the bed. Gripping Lludd's upper arms, Archer dug in and did his best to stay still.

"Do it," Archer urged when he sensed Lludd's hesitation.

Lludd did. He tore through Archer's jeans, taking Archer's underwear with it. As Lludd drew away, sliding down his body, he used his other hand on the other side. Soon, every stitch of clothing Archer had been wearing lay in tattered pieces on either side and beneath him.

Kneeling between Archer's thighs, Lludd peered down at him appreciatively. "Oh, my mate," he rumbled, skimming the claws of his index finger up and down Archer's straining erection, ever-so-lightly. "Thing of beauty. Can't wait to taste it, to feel it moving within me." Flicking his gaze to Archer's, he snarled, "Mine."

Archer grinned up at him, whispering, "I want it to be yours, but I see one little problem."

Lludd's eyes narrowed. "What problem?"

Pointing at Lludd's groin, Archer stated, "You're over-dressed."

Hissing, Lludd grabbed the stays of his loincloth with his free hand. With a practiced-looking motion, the gargoyle swiped the bit of fabric from his hips and tossed it aside.

Archer sucked in a harsh breath as he took in Lludd's massive erection. It was even bigger than he'd thought upon feeling it. He licked his lips as he admired the gargoyle's dark-purple, probably eleven-inch erection. Lludd's foreskin had pulled back, revealing his damp head and oozing slit. The cock twitched before Archer's eyes.

Snapping his focus back to Lludd's face, Archer gave his gargoyle a lazy smile. He reached down and gripped his own dick. "Not bad, Lludd," Archer murmured huskily. "I sure hope you know how to use it."

Lludd growled low in his throat. "Oh, I do, trouble-maker."

Grinning, Archer reached down and cradled his own balls. He tugged his dick with his other hand while spreading his legs wide.

"I'm sure I have absolutely no idea what you mean."

To Archer's pleasure, Lludd let out a hungry snarl, batted his hands away, then swallowed his dick to the root.

Arching with delight, Archer groaned Lludd's name.

CHAPTER TEN

A rcher's flavor burst across Lludd's tongue, causing his mouth to water for more. Swiping along his turgid flesh, he took in the pleasant flavors of light salt and male musk. He inhaled deeply, causing his senses to reel.

Then Archer's pre-cum hit his tongue, and he groaned.

Lludd felt his own erection twitch and throb between his thighs. Groaning at the sensation, feeling Archer's dick answer with another bead of pre-cum, he knew his lover — his one and only — was just as close as he was. While thinking was difficult, and Lludd truly wanted to taste Archer's fluids, he knew they both needed to take the edge off.

Plus, we'll have plenty of time for exploration if we're not clamoring for release.

Still, pulling off Archer's tasty cock was one of the hardest things Lludd had ever done. Hearing his mate's whine of dismay didn't help. He crooned in reassurance as he levered over his human.

"Easy, Archer," Lludd rumbled. "I have you, my mate."

"I was so damn close," Archer grumbled.

Lludd chuckled as he grinned down at him. "Not stopping." Then he lowered his hips and slotted his longer, thicker erection against Archer's perfectly proportioned one. "Just something to take the edge off."

Then Lludd gripped his foreskin and eased it over Archer's crown. From the first feel of his mate's flared head sliding against his own more sensitive crown, a hard shudder rocked through him. He barely heard Archer's swiftly indrawn breath.

Feeling the slight shiver in the body beneath him as well as the whimpering moan from Archer, Lludd forced himself to pull it together. He gripped their shafts and squeezed, pressing them together tightly. Then Lludd began a subtle, gentle rocking.

Being docked together in such a fashion, Lludd knew it wouldn't take long. His crown was too damn sensitive. Knowing Archer had been right on the edge, he figured his human would lose it soon, too.

Lludd rubbed their dicks together, their crowns sliding against each other, and held their stalks tightly flushed. Lowering his head, he sucked on Archer's flesh where he longed to sink his teeth. He reveled in the sounds of Archer's pleasure and the way his fingernails dug into his arms as he clung to him.

Perfect. So damn perfect.

"L-Lludd!" Archer cried, trembling beneath him. "O-Oh, o-oh, f-fuck!"

To his satisfaction, Lludd felt Archer shudder against him. He felt the cock against his own twitch, swelling within his grip. Then the warm cream of Archer's release oozed over his sensitive crown.

Moaning against Archer's shoulder, Lludd let his swell of need crest. His balls pulled tight, and he jerked and shuddered as he poured out his seed. He groaned with satisfaction, knowing he mingled his essence with Archer's own.

When the endorphins from Lludd's orgasm finally began to wane, he sighed deeply. He kissed Archer's neck once more before forcing coordination into his body. Ever-so-gently, he levered up a little and eased his foreskin upward, separating their pricks.

Even the slight sting of separation was more than worth the ecstasy he'd just experienced.

"Damn," Archer muttered, peering up at him. He licked

his lips. "That was—Never done that, I—" Archer seemed to run out of words, and he just grinned somewhat loopily at him.

Chuckling huskily, Lludd dipped his head and pecked a kiss to his lips. "That's just to take the edge off, my mate."

Archer snorted as he shook his head. "I know over forty isn't old to you guys, but to humans, it means my days of getting it up a second time in one night are over." He sighed deeply, grinning. "Not that experiencing that wasn't totally worth it."

"Hmm, I accept your challenge," Lludd mused as he took in his relaxed human. He smirked as he reached over and grabbed the lube someone had oh-so-helpfully left on the nightstand. Rocking back to sit on his calves, Lludd began to remove the plastic. "Then I'll just clean you up"—he gave Archer a lascivious smile—"with my tongue, while opening your chute to take my cock."

Archer's eyes widened, and his gaze drifted to Lludd's jutting erection. "Damn," he whispered. "You're still hard."

Smirking, Lludd skimmed his forefinger up Archer's dick, watching it twitch while bringing his mate's attention to his still-randy state. "You are, too, my mate," he pointed out with a wink. "Now let me clean you."

"O-Oh, shit."

Grinning upon hearing Archer's shock-filled whispered words, Lludd put word to deed. He opened his mouth, stuck out his tongue, and swiped over his crown and abs, scooping up their combined fluids where they'd dripped along his erection and over his abdominals. As Lludd did that, he popped the cap on the lube and poured a liberal amount on his fingertips. Just as Archer began to wiggle beneath his ministrations, huffing and grunting as he gripped the comforter beneath them, Lludd tossed the closed tube aside and used the hand to grip his hips.

"Relax," Lludd crooned. "I'll take such good care of you, my mate."

"God, your mouth feels amazing," Archer mumbled, twitching in his hold. "What you do to me."

"Is give you pleasure, Archer," Lludd murmured as he lowered his lubed fingers and teased his slick fingers around and around his mate's hole. "Always and so much pleasure."

"Yesssss," Archer growled, spreading his legs wider. "More."

Lludd slid his finger into Archer's channel, more than on board with that. At the same time, he licked up the last of their seed which had spilled onto his mate. He was adding a second finger an instant later, and he paused, realizing how loose his mate actually was. For an instant, jealousy ripped through Lludd, making him freeze in his ministrations.

"Nooooo," Archer whined. "Don't stop." He squeezed and released on Lludd's embedded fingers. "Your fingers are so much better than any toy."

Forcing himself to move once more, Lludd smiled against Archer's stomach muscles. "Have you been playing with yourself, while thinking of me?" He flicked his gaze upward, taking in Archer's flushed face and heaving torso.

"Yessss," Archer admitted roughly. "This is so much better."

Instantly, Lludd's ire dissolved, leaving behind only simmering arousal. His cock throbbed, and he pressed a third finger into his mate. To Lludd's pleasure, Archer sighed deeply, staying loose.

Still, Lludd knew he needed to stretch him with one more finger in order to take him safely.

"Need you," Archer urged, gripping Lludd's upper arms and tugging. "Please, Lludd."

Lludd met Archer's gaze, taking in the gorgeous sight of need darkening his mate's green eyes. "Just one more,

Archer," he murmured, nuzzling his mate's straining erection. "Don't wanna hurt you."

Then Lludd suckled on Archer's crown and frenulum as he began to slowly wedge his fourth digit into his lover. Finally, he felt his mate begin to stiffen. He opened his mouth and swallowed Archer to the root.

Archer gasped, a shudder working through him.

Lludd sucked strongly as he eased partway off Archer's prick. As soon as he reached the top, he scraped his canine over his mate's frenulum, relishing the howling mewl drawn from his human's throat. Lludd would have worried he'd hurt his mate, but the shudder of his body and the bead of pre-cum that coated his tongue told him differently.

Sure, there might have been pain, but Archer evidently loved it.

As Lludd repeated the actions, he curled his fingers upward and pressed against Archer's prostate. He gently rubbed that inner nub, stimulating inside and out. His mate began to babble his name, chanting *more* and *now* and *Lludd*. Taking advantage of his human being out of his mind, he continued to stretch his mate's chute.

By the time Lludd felt no more tension in Archer's body, his mate staying pliant and begging beneath him, Lludd's balls were practically drawn tightly against him. He knew he needed to get balls deep right then or he would have to start all over again later.

Lludd had no intention of doing that.

Easing his fingers free of Archer, Lludd popped off his dick, drawing a whimper from his blissed-out mate. He gripped his lover's hips and lifted, then easily flipped the man. Hearing Archer's indrawn breath, Lludd paused and scented the air.

Did I draw blood?

While Lludd didn't smell any, he feared he'd injured his human in another way. Rubbing his palm up his spine, he crooned, "You okay, my mate?'

"Oh, yeah," Archer immediately replied before chuckling huskily. "So fucking sexy how you can move me around." He peered over his shoulder at Lludd, his expression open and honest and his eyes widely dilated. "Love it."

Growling with feral delight, Lludd rumbled, "Good." He pushed closer to Archer. He pressed his straining erection against Archer's crack as he used his knees to push his human's wider. "Gonna shove you around a lot if you keep responding like this."

Archer returned his focus to the bed. At the same time, he arched his back and pressed against his groin. "Yesss, Lludd," he urged, pulling away and rocking against him again. "More. Make me yours."

"You're already mine," Lludd declared as he grabbed the lube and poured some directly onto his dick. He hissed at the cool sensation as he popped the tube closed. After tossing it aside, Lludd slicked himself. "Now and forever."

Without another word, Lludd pressed the head of his erection to Archer's prepared hole and pushed. He groaned as his mate's body opened to him, allowing his crown to be engulfed in bliss-inducing heat and pressure. Hearing Archer moan, feeling the tension in his body, Lludd froze.

Lludd draped over Archer's back, resting his weight on his left hand. Reaching under his human, he rubbed over his taut abdominals. At the same time, he licked and nuzzled the stretch of skin he longed to mark.

"Easy, my mate," Lludd crooned. "Breathe for me. Relax."

Archer hummed and turned his head. "I'm okay," he whispered with a kiss to Lludd's temple. "You're big, but I'm ready. I wanna feel all of you."

Gauging the pressure around his crown for an instant, Lludd realized Archer had indeed already relaxed. He did as his mate wanted and thrust. Sinking deep into his forever lover in one long slow glide, Lludd gritted his teeth at the exquisite sensations caressing his length.

Once Lludd bottomed out, he groaned low in his throat. "Oh, Archer, my mate," he ground out. "You feel so damn good."

"Y-You too," Archer said around panting breaths. "God, you stretch me so perfectly. Feel so good."

"This will feel even better," Lludd vowed.

Then Lludd began moving. He eased his erection slowly out until his crown stretched Archer's ring. Switching directions, he sank back into his mate just as slowly. As Lludd continued with the slow long-dicking of his mate, reveling in the hot cocoon of his human's body, he searched for that perfect spot.

Several times, Archer tried to push against him, trying to get him to speed up. "Faster, damn it," he demanded, trembling in Lludd's hold.

"Not, yet, mate," Lludd declared, his voice raspy with his carefully restrained need. "Waited so long to enjoy my mate for the first time." He nipped at Archer's earlobe, then suckled lightly before whispering, "Gonna savor you all night long."

Archer groaned even as he relaxed into Lludd's ministrations. A couple of thrusts later, he gasped, then moaned louder as a hard shudder worked through his body.

Lludd hummed. "Found it," he muttered against the flesh of Archer's neck, a satisfied grin curving his lips.

Moving his lips down to where he intended to bite, he began sucking up a mark. He sped up his strokes, slowly at first, then faster. All the while, he continued to nail that ecstasy-giving spot hidden inside his mate.

"Lludd. Lludd, please. Need," Archer babbled. "Need, oh fuck! G-Gonna. So close. I—"

Loving having reduced his mate to one-word sentences, Lludd slid his right hand down Archer's torso and wrapped his fingers around his prick. He tightened his grip and jacked him. Two strokes was all it took.

Archer cried his pleasure. His body jolted spastically beneath Lludd. His cum covered his fingers and the comforter beneath them.

Lludd gritted his teeth as he continued to rut into Archer. Pegging his prostate over and over, he did his best to extend his mate's pleasure. Finally, the tight squeeze to the sensitive skin of his erection overwhelmed him, and Lludd could no longer hold back.

With his orgasm barreling through him, Lludd roared. His hips jerked once, twice, before he buried himself as deeply as he could, pouring his seed into Archer's body. He clutched his mate close to him, flushing his chest to his human's back.

Giving in to his instincts, Lludd opened his mouth and struck. He sank his sharp teeth into Archer's flesh, causing blood to ooze around them. The iron-rich flavor burst across his tongue, making his taste buds sing.

Lludd moaned and swallowed, reveling in the sweet nectar that was his mate's life-giving fluid. Sucking hard on the wound, he lashed his tongue around his embedded teeth, scooping more blood into his mouth. He swallowed that too before going back for more.

Archer whimpered in Lludd's hold, but the feel of his mate's chute clenching and releasing around his prick, still encased in his body's sweet heat, told him the reason. His mate was coming once more. The exquisite scent of Archer's cum again flooded the room.

Smug satisfaction filling him, Lludd eased his teeth from Archer's flesh. He carefully licked over his mark. In seconds, the skin healed, leaving a beautiful claiming scar behind.

"Gorgeous," Lludd whispered. "My mark."

When Archer didn't respond, Lludd lifted up a little. He

cradled his human's jaw and urged him to turn his head a little. What he saw made him grin.

Archer snored softly, his face lax, his expression sated.

"Also gorgeous."

Lludd leaned down and pecked a kiss to the corner of Archer's mouth. After carefully easing out of his mate's body, he settled his man on the bed, making certain he wasn't in the wet spot. Unmindful of his still hard dick, Lludd headed to the ensuite.

After washing himself, hissing once or twice due to sensitivity, Lludd returned to Archer's side. He wiped down his mate, cleaning him of lube and seed. When Archer moaned softly and mumbled in his sleep, Lludd grinned, pleased his lover was rousing.

After tossing the dirty cloth onto the bathroom floor, Lludd returned to his snoozing mate. He eased back onto the bed and grabbed the discarded lube. Grinning wickedly, he swept his gaze over his sexy naked lover.

Time to wake him up for another round.

Lludd popped the cap and poured a dollop onto his tail. Closing it and placing it aside, he returned to between Archer's thighs. As he began licking his mate's half-hard dick, stimulating it and urging it back to full arousal, Lludd slid his tail into his own chute and began stretching himself.

After only a moment, Archer threaded his fingers into Lludd's hair and moaned his name.

Peering through his lashes at his lover, Lludd met Archer's gaze. He saw the lust in his human's green orbs and grinned around his mouthful of meat.

Oh, yeah. Time to complete our bond.

CHAPTER ELEVEN

"You've had a perpetual smile on your face for three days. It's disgusting."

Archer lifted his focus from his paperwork and met Geraldo's gaze. The big deputy was leaning against the doorframe. His expression appeared anything but disgusted.

Geraldo grinned widely at him.

Unable to help himself, Archer smiled back. "Can't help it. Being in love will do that to a man." Realizing what he'd said, his brows shot up. "Well, damn." Concern shot through him, and his smile slipped from his lips.

"Being well-sexed will do that to a man, too," Geraldo commented with a snort.

Archer scoffed, not bothering to deign to answer that comment.

Geraldo's eyes narrowed. "And now you look troubled." He tilted his head. "It happened when you talked about being in love. So what? What's the trouble? Don't think Lludd loves you back?"

"Oh, I'm sure he does," Archer replied quickly. Then amended, "Or will be soon. He's definitely smitten. I just . . . isn't it too fast?"

"How long have you been seeing him?"

Hesitating, Archer tried to decide on the truth or not. Even learning that gargoyles could impregnate their male mates with an egg hadn't caused so much unease in him. "Um, a week?"

Geraldo's jaw sagged open. Then he snapped it closed and

gave a half-shrug. "I hear sometimes it happens fast." A wistful smile curved his thick lips. "I know if I found someone who made me light up like Lludd does for you, I'd dive in with both feet." Blinking once, Geraldo cleared his expression and once again pasted on his happy-go-lucky smile. "Sometimes you just know, man."

Archer nodded, pushing his fears aside for another time. "So, did you stop by for something specific? What are you doing here?" Grimacing, he asked, "Another double shift?"

Nodding, Geraldo admitted, "Keith called in. His wife went into labor."

"Damn, okay. Thanks for filling in again." Archer tapped the end of his pen on his desk. "Let's set up a collection fund for the new baby. Should have done that before."

With being so busy and short-handed, there were things that had fallen through the cracks.

"Already done, boss," Geraldo stated with a grin. "That's why I'm here. How much should I write you down for?" His smile dimmed. "And we received another anonymous tip about the Lindson ranch. You've been out there twice. What is the tipster seeing that you aren't?"

"Put me in for two hundred." Archer answered Geraldo's first question. Then he rubbed his chin. "Actually, I'm inclined to think someone is either trying to waste our time to keep us from looking into other things, or someone has a grudge against them and is hoping I find something to cause problems for the ranch." Shaking his head, Archer added, "Either way, it won't work. Lludd works there. It's where I met him."

Geraldo's eyes widened, and a shit-eating grin curved his lips. "Oh, damn. Getting in good with the rich cattle baron, eh?" He waggled his dark eyebrows. "Nice!" Then he sobered. "Next time, I'm going to tell the tipster that they either have to come in person and explain specifically what they saw, or they have to provide us with photos. Maybe that will deter them."

"Hope so." Archer watched as Geraldo turned, then called, "Oh, hey. Our new staff will start next week. It'll be nice having another couple pairs of hands."

Pausing, Geraldo looked over his shoulder. "That is good news."

"I'm going to pair you up with Marco, and I'll pair Margo up with Sandro. Hopefully, they'll pick everything up quickly."

Archer had been assured by Bodb that Sandro wouldn't need but a day to get up to speed, but at least a week was standard procedure.

Geraldo crossed his fingers. "Here's to hopin'." Then he disappeared out of Archer's view.

Returning to his paperwork, Archer finished a report on a break-in at the corner gas station. He'd discovered prints that belonged to a man on the run from the police department in Houston. After sending his findings to the detective in charge there, he pulled up another file.

Before Archer could dive into it, his phone rang. "Yes, Marinette?" he asked, greeting the woman at the front desk.

"Sheriff Montgomery," she greeted him formally. "Mayor Loreman is here to see you."

Archer tightened his left hand into a fist as he licked his lips. He'd been expecting the mayor's visit ever since he sent out the notices to the applicants who didn't get the job that morning. He figured Darcy had run right to daddy and complained.

"Of course, Marin," Archer replied. "Grab Geraldo and have him escort Mayor Loreman to me."

"Yes, Sheriff." Then she disconnected.

Grabbing his phone, Archer tapped in a quick message to Lludd.

Mayor's here. Ten minutes later than I expected. LOL.

Archer knew Lludd was hanging around in town with Bodb, Nicholas, Attain, and Ssimeas. They planned to kill two birds with one stone. With the mayor at the station, his lover would drop by to take him to lunch.

Out myself while letting the mayor know that there is no way his son will get a job here. This'll be fun.

The beep of his phone caught his attention, and he checked it to see a thumbs-up emoji from Lludd.

Smiling, Archer set his phone aside and turned his attention to the doorway.

A second later, Geraldo knocked on the doorframe.

Archer beckoned. "Come in, too, Geraldo." He wanted a witness, just in case the mayor decided to threaten him.

Geraldo nodded and moved to sit in the corner.

Rising, Archer greeted the mayor, holding his hand out over his desk. "Hello, Mayor Loreman. Always good to see you," he lied. After shaking the mayor's hand, and fighting back a cringe at how soft and slightly damp the overweight man's hand was, Archer indicated the chair before his desk. "What can I help you with today?"

As if I don't already know.

After taking a seat, Mayor Loreman glanced Geraldo's way disdainfully before stating, "I'd like to speak with you in private."

Yep, the apple doesn't fall far from the tree.

Archer knew the mayor's order was clear. Have Geraldo leave.

Not happening.

"May I ask a frank question, Mayor Loreman?" Archer decided to cut right to the chase.

Curving his lips into an insincere smile, Mayor Loreman nodded. "Of course."

"Is this conversation about why I did not hire your son, Deputy Darcy Loreman, for one of the open positions at my station?"

The mayor's eyes narrowed just a smidge, and his lips pinched. "Why would you think that was why I would come by today?"

That's not a no.

Archer kept his expression blank. "There are several reasons, actually. First, I sent out the notices to those who did not get the position this morning." He lifted a second finger. "Second, when I interviewed Deputy Loreman, he acted as if he already had the job and didn't take the interview seriously." When the mayor opened his mouth, Archer hurried to continue with, "Finally, my father called me and let me know that *you*'d called *him* and asked him to *impress* the importance of allowing your son to work closer to home."

Knowing the mayor would drop by, Archer had talked with his father. He'd confirmed that Marshal didn't mind if Archer told the mayor about how he'd called him. "After all," his father had said. "I'm retired and have plenty of friends, too. He can't do anything to me."

Lifting his chin, Mayor Loreman stated, "Very well. Yes, I have come to speak with you about your decision." He flicked his gaze toward Geraldo once more, a barely disguised sneer on his face. "Which is why I'd like to speak with you privately."

"Deputy Martinez aided me in the selection process," Archer stated coolly. He relaxed back in his chair, placed his elbows on the armrests, and tee-peed his fingers before him. "If you have a problem with our decision, then he should be here to hear it."

Mayor Loreman's nostrils flared, and his expression could only be called scandalized. "You allowed *him* to choose your new deputies?"

"To help me, yes," Archer corrected calmly. "He's been here longest save for me, knows our current people and how they work together, and his insight on how each of the applicants would mesh with us here is invaluable."

The mayor glanced at Geraldo again. His face flushed, and he turned beady eyes on Archer. "Why didn't my son get the job, Sheriff? Who could possibly have been a better fit? Darcy grew up in this town. He knows the people."

It seemed all pretense was being dropped.

Good.

Leaning forward, Archer rested his forearms on his desk. "I did take that into consideration, Mayor Loreman." He folded his hands, so he didn't make fists as he continued, "It was also one of the reasons I disqualified him."

"What?" The mayor sounded outraged. "That's ridiculous. It would aid him in our need to clean up the streets and get rid of the riff-raff pervading our town."

Archer frowned, unable to help himself. That comment was interesting. "Our crime rate is extremely low, mayor," he pointed out. "What riff-raff would you be speaking of?"

Sniffing disdainfully, Mayor Loreman stated, "If you don't recognize it, perhaps you're part of the problem."

"Another reason I chose not to hire Deputy Loreman, is because his current supervisor has marked in his file several instances of excessive force." Archer chose to ignore the mayor's comment. He knew they would end up addressing that before too long. "The last one just recently, and he's been ordered to go through an anger management course as well as a sensitivity training. If I hired him here right now, he would get out of it. I didn't think that would be a benefit for him."

Mayor Loreman's knuckles turned white as he gripped his chair arms tightly. "You and that bastard he currently works under are sabotaging my son's career," he accused. "Those incidents were blown completely out of proportion."

"Mayor Loreman." Archer hardened his voice. "I was thinking of what was *best* for your son's career when I chose not to hire him. He needs to learn control and acceptance of those different than him." He could see the mayor building up another head of steam to say more, his face turning red and his eyes narrowing, so Archer did his best to head it off at the pass. "Besides, there were other more qualified applicants to the positions." Rising from his seat, Archer stated, "I'm sorry your son won't be closer to home at this time." As much it galled him to say it, Archer knew the proper way to end the conversation with the mayor. "Encourage Deputy Loreman to apply again the next time we have an opening."

Archer prayed that wouldn't be for a long, long time.

Mayor Loreman didn't rise. Instead, he leaned back in his seat and frowned at him. His expression appeared . . . petulant.

Damn, acting like a child when he isn't getting his way.

"Was there something else, Mayor?" Archer asked placidly.

"I want to see the files on these two men that you think are better than my son," the mayor demanded.

Shaking his head, Archer replied, "I'm sorry, Mayor Loreman, but you know that's classified."

Mayor Loreman finally rose from his chair. "This isn't over, Archer," he claimed disrespectfully. "My son *will* be in this department, make no mistake of that." With that, the mayor turned and strode swiftly out of the office.

"That sounded like a threat," Geraldo muttered as he rose.

"Yep, and after what's coming next, I'm sure he'll be damn overt about it."

Geraldo frowned. "Next?"

Archer beckoned. "Yup. Wanna meet Lludd?"

"Hell, yeah."

Leaving his office with Geraldo following close behind, Archer easily caught up with the mayor, since he walked with a stiff, pompous stride. He looked beyond the mayor and spotted almost half a dozen people in the waiting area. Lludd stood at the counter, speaking with Marinette.

As if recognizing that Archer had appeared, Lludd peered

past her and met his eyes. He grinned.

Archer couldn't help but grin back. He took his time admiring his gargoyle's human form. While he thought Lludd as a gargoyle was sexy—he loved exploring his man's wings, and when he'd discovered the leathery appendages were a hot spot for the gargoyle, did it often—Lludd as a human was just as hot.

Lludd lost about six inches of height, leaving him at six-foot-six. His medium-purple hide turned to deep brown skin. Since his long, dark-gray hair didn't change, Lludd had it pulled back in a queue, accentuating his square-jawed features. He had broad shoulders, thickly muscled limbs, and a trim waist with a six-pack.

Knowing Lludd didn't understand human aesthetics just made it better, because he was completely oblivious to his own appeal.

Archer hadn't realized he had a jealous bone until he'd heard Stanley wolf whistle the first time the foreman had seen Lludd's human form. He'd wanted to gouge the Native American's eyes out of his head. Archer hadn't been able to stop his growl.

Stanley had lifted his hands and told him, "I'd never try to poach, Sheriff." Then he winked. "Besides, paranormals never stray. People can look, but the paranormal will never let them touch."

Lludd had wrapped his arm around Archer's waist and pulled him close to his side. After pecking his temple, he'd rumbled, "Stanley is right. I'll never get it up for anyone but you."

"Oh, Sheriff. I was about to call you." Marinette's voice drew Archer out of the memory. "This man says he's here to take you to lunch?" She sounded uncertain.

Archer nodded. "Hello, handsome," he greeted Lludd.

As expected, Mayor Loreman stopped where he had been

passing Lludd's group. He spun around, a scowl etched on his features.

Ignoring him, Archer reached over and squeezed Lludd's upper arm. "Lludd, I'd like you to meet Deputy Gerome Martinez. He helps me run the place."

"Nice to meet you, Lludd." Gerome held out his hand. "Loved that sappy note you wrote."

Lludd's dark cheeks probably hid his blush, but he muttered, "I had a lot of help with it."

Gerome stepped back as he nodded. "Well, the smile on the sheriff's face is real nice to see, so keep up the good work." Then his eyes narrowed. "Be warned. If you break his heart, there are a lot of overprotective deputies here that will make your life miserable."

Marinette gasped. "Lludd is your man, Sheriff?" She grinned widely, finally catching on. "So this is the guy who's been putting that smile on your face."

Archer nodded. "He sure is." As much as he wanted to, he resisted kissing Lludd right there in front of everyone. He had to have some decorum, after all.

"You're a faggot?" the mayor roared, drawing everyone's attention.

"Well, that's not a very nice thing to say, Mayor," Nicholas commented, crossing his arms over his chest as he pinned a narrow-eyed gaze on the man. "Didn't know you were a bigot."

Sneering at Nicholas, Mayor Loreman snapped, "You're a disgrace to the Lindson family." Then he turned his attention to Archer and pointed at him. "I'm calling for a revote. Enjoy your last days as sheriff. No one in this town is going to keep a faggot in office."

With that parting shot, Mayor Loreman stormed out of the station.

"Well, that was about as dramatic as I thought it'd be,"

Archer commented. He smiled at Geraldo and Marinette. "I'm headed to lunch with my man. I'll be back in a bit."

Acting as if he didn't have a care in the world, he headed out with the others for a lunch date.

Gods, I hope this idea doesn't go tits up.

Still, Archer would give up anything to stay with his gargoyle.

CHAPTER TWELVE

L ludd sat on the roof of the barn and watched the figure creep along the fence line. Whoever it was, female considering the size, was obviously trying not to be seen. He decided to suggest surveillance cameras along the driveway.

Hmm . . . where did she park?

Learning from his mistakes, Lludd pulled out his phone. Ducking behind the cupola of the barn, he quickly dimmed the backlighting on his phone. Then he typed a message to Gladstone. Biscane was enjoying a well-deserved night off.

Female intruder creeping along the driveway toward the main house. I have eyes on her. Will you find her vehicle and see if registration has identity?

A second later, Lludd received a reply.

On it, brother.

Then Lludd sent a text to Bodb.

Another intruder. Female this time. Will apprehend. Bring her to you?

Lludd peered around the cupola and zeroed in on the figure. The light of the quarter moon glinted off something in her hands, and he squinted.

What is that?

Feeling his phone vibrate in his hand, Lludd returned to his hiding spot and read the text from Bodb.

If you can do it in human form.

Smirking, Lludd typed a quick response.

Will do.

Then Lludd clipped the phone to the holder attached to his

belt. He was in his true form, but he still wore jeans. After a few dates in town with Archer, Lludd figured he might as well get used to them. Plus, he'd found that he was only one waist-size smaller in his human form, so he could wear jeans in his natural form, then tighten his belt a hole if he needed to change shape.

Lludd watched the woman's trajectory, seeing that she was bypassing the front barn in favor of heading toward the foaling barn. Once she'd passed his position, he dropped to the ground on the opposite side. After shifting to human form, Lludd tightened his belt to keep his pants up, before padding on bare feet to the edge of the structure.

Even in human form, Lludd still had better-than-average eyesight. He spotted the woman stop at the door, glance around, then slip inside. Sprinting across the expanse, he paused at the door.

The light was still off, but he could see the gleam around the edges, probably from a flashlight.

Taking a deep breath, Lludd opened the door and stepped inside. Even before he saw her, he stated gruffly, "You're trespassing, lady. What are you doing here?"

The woman's gasp helped him zero in on the woman. She stood halfway down the aisle near a stall door. In one hand she carried the flashlight, and in the other, she held . . . a camera.

Huh?

Striding forward, Lludd gave her a stern look. "Who are you, and what are you doing here?"

She backed up one step, two, all the while glancing around as if searching for some avenue of escape. Then she turned and rushed toward the door at the other end of the building.

Sighing, Lludd rolled his eyes as he gave chase. He reached her just as she did the door. Lludd had just enough time to yank her out of the way of the opening door. Otherwise, it would have nailed her in the face.

She screamed.

Lludd slapped a hand over her mouth, stopping the offending noise.

Stanley flicked on the lights. His black eyebrows shot up, and he glanced between them. "Lludd?"

The woman turned her face just enough to holler a muffled, "Help! He attacked me!"

"Hey, Stanley," Lludd grumbled. "She crept onto the grounds with a camera. If you don't scream, lady, I'll let your mouth go."

Crossing his arms over his chest, Stanley stated, "I saw a weird light coming from here, so I thought I'd check it out. Can't be too careful during fire season." He scowled at the woman. "So, who are you, and what are you doing here?"

Lludd removed his hand, but she remained mutinously silent.

Stanley shrugged while Lludd rolled his eyes. The foreman held the door open.

"Let's go," Lludd ordered, pushing her out the door.

"Hey, Lludd! Just a sec!"

Lludd peered to the right and spotted Virgil jogging toward him. "Do you know her?"

Virgil swept his gaze over the woman. "Naw, but here ya go." He dropped something at Lludd's feet. "Bare feet on gravel sucks."

Peering downward, Lludd chuckled upon spotting the pair of flip-flops. "Thanks, Virg."

After passing the woman off to Stanley, Lludd thrust his feet into them. Then he led the way across the gravel area to the back deck. Reaching the back door, he opened it and led the way inside.

Lludd entered the dining room and found several people milling about. Bodb sat at the head of the table with Nicholas to his right — the elder with his nightly tumbler of tequila and his mate with a beer. Lebone leaned against the wall near the dining room door with his arms crossed over his chest. Spieron and Albert were at the table, too, a glass of red wine in front of each.

Moving the woman to a seat across from Spieron and a few down, Lludd forced her into the seat.

She glared at everyone but kept her silence.

Upon seeing Bodb's arched brow, Lludd shrugged. "She was in the foaling barn with a camera." He placed the device on the table. "Not sure what she was looking for. She hasn't said much."

"What's your name?" Elder Bodb asked, his voice demanding answers.

She trembled, but to her credit, she didn't speak.

Huh.

"Her name is Agatha Drismel." Gladstone's voice came from the front room, announcing his presence. He appeared a second later, carrying a few pieces of paper and a purse. "She's twenty-seven years old, lives in the West Court Trailer Park, and drives an oh-seven *Camry.*" His brother's dark-brown eyes narrowed as he pinned a disgusted look on Agatha. "She has a car seat in the back that would fit a cub of about three or four." Shaking his head, Gladstone asked, "You leave your kid home with a sitter so you can sneak around our ranch? Why?"

Once more, Agatha stubbornly refused to answer.

"I've called the sheriff," Bodb announced before he lifted his drink to his lips and took a sip.

Nicholas added, "You may as well tell us. Were you the one behind the anonymous tips about shady dealings?"

Agatha's scent of unease answered for her.

Lludd tipped his chin in a slight nod even as his body reacted to the news that his sheriff was on his way over.

Sighing, Lludd headed to the sideboard. "If you don't want to tell me what you want to drink, I'll just bring you a bottle of water, Agatha," he told her. At the same time, he grabbed a beer for himself from one of the mini-fridges. Since she didn't answer, Lludd took a sealed bottle of water from a different fridge and placed it in front of her.

Then . . . they waited in silence.

Twenty minutes later, Lludd heard the crunch of tires on gravel. His heart rate spiked as anticipation filled him. He couldn't help the way his prick thickened, but at least, the jeans hid it better than the loincloth would have.

Lludd thought Sheriff Archer Montgomery looked damn fantastic in his uniform.

Even better out of it.

Controlling those thoughts were tough as Lludd watched his sheriff enter the dining room—escorted by Gladstone—and peer around the room. He surveyed the room for a second, his gaze lingering on Lludd and his lips twitched just a smidge, acknowledging him. Then his focus landed on Agatha.

Archer rested his fists on his hips as he pinned a displeased gaze on Agatha. "Agatha, what the hell?" He shook his head and didn't wait for her to respond. "Is this because of Henry?"

"Henry?" Stanley latched onto that. "Do you mean the asshole who attacked Shaw in the men's room at Landry's bar?"

Nodding, Archer pointed at Agatha. "This is his sister. Henry supported her and her daughter because she doesn't work." Lifting his gaze to the ceiling, his human appeared to be counting to three as if to calm his temper. Finally, Archer frowned at Agatha once more. "What the hell were you thinking? What do you think will happen to Lenora if you're kicked out of the trailer park? She'll be taken from you. Is that what you want?"

"That wouldn't even have been a possibility until these assholes lied about what happened in the bathroom and had him sent to prison," Agatha screamed, jumping from the table.

"These faggot assholes are to blame for everything!"

Well, that sounds extreme.

Lludd moved to put himself between Agatha and those at the head of the table.

Spieron, however, rapped his knuckles on the table, drawing Agatha's attention. His eyes were already hazed, the vampire's irises blood-red against his black pupils. As soon as he caught her gaze, she stilled, her features slackening.

"Well, that's sort of freaky," Archer murmured.

"Spieron's abilities are definitely useful at times," Bodb commented, casting a smile the sheriff's way. Then he refocused on Spieron. "So, she blames us for having her brother sent to jail, and since Henry was her cash cow, even if a poor one, the idea of supporting herself has sent her off the deep end."

Cocking his head, Spieron narrowed his eyes. "Hmmm, it seems she's under the impression that if she discredits those at the ranch, the charges against Henry will be dropped." He shook his head as he pinned his red-eyed gaze Bodb's way. "Then things will" — he lifted his fingers in air quotes — "go back to the way things should be. Her brother supporting her and her child."

"Out of curiosity," Archer cut in. "Who is Lenora's father?'

Spieron stared at Agatha for a moment, then turned his attention to Archer. "She really doesn't know." He winced. "Let's just say she wasn't too discerning while under the influence of alcohol."

Bodb sighed deeply as he met Nicholas's gaze. "What do you want to do?"

Nicholas rubbed the back of his neck. "I'd say we should ask Shaw and Virgil, but I don't want her making trouble for our place anymore."

"We heard." Shaw stepped from the shadow of the hall that led to the mudroom at the back door.

Virgil appeared next to him, wrapping his arm around his

mate's waist. "We'd rather not take a cub from her mother if said mother can be . . . rehabilitated."

Shaw nodded emphatically even as his focus riveted on Agatha. "Can she suddenly have an epiphany that she's better off? Maybe that her brother's influence and his drinking were a bad example for her and her daughter?"

"Could she become a good mother and a useful member of society?" Virgil posited. "Get a job. Take care of herself. Take care of Lenora?"

Spieron hummed as he pinned his focus on Agatha again. For several long moments, no one said a word.

Lludd couldn't help himself. As he waited, he crossed the few feet separating them and wrapped Archer in his arms. He pressed a slow, sipping kiss to his lips, and soon lost himself in the action of kissing his mate.

"If you want to come up for air any time soon, I'll tell the sheriff what we can expect from Agatha in the future."

Spieron's amused voice broke into Lludd's make-out session. He felt his mate groan as he pressed his forehead into the crook of his neck. His sheriff's hat fell to the floor, and Lludd clutched him close as he rubbed his hands up and down his back.

For good measure, Lludd glared at the vampire

Too bad Spieron seemed completely unfazed, smirking back at him.

Lludd suddenly realized that Agatha was gone, as was Gladstone. "What'd I miss?"

Several in the room chuckled, but Bodb answered. "Gladstone is taking Agatha back to her sedan." His smile turned sad. "We'll keep an eye on her." Then Bodb focused on Archer, who'd lifted his head and turned to face the elder. "She shouldn't be calling in any more anonymous tips to your office or be causing any more trouble for the ranch." Bodb snorted before he stated, "Evidently, she'd called in a tip this evening, but whoever was in charge told her that they'd searched multiple times and would either need her to come down to explain in detail or they would need pictures."

Archer chuckled softly. "That would have been Geraldo. He's on night duty for the most part, but he's been taking an occasional double shift when needed." He shook his head. "Can't wait for the new guys to get up to speed."

"Me, too," Lludd cut in, rubbing up and down his mate's back. "I hate how tired you always are."

Shrugging, Archer warned, "It's the nature of the job, Lludd. Sometimes, there will be long hours."

Lludd nodded, understanding. "And I'll always be there to support and take care of you."

Archer's relieved smile curved his features, and Lludd couldn't help but taste that.

Except, a few seconds after Lludd had pushed his tongue into Archer's mouth, his mate turned his head, breaking the kiss. "Wait, wait," he grumbled, scowling at him. "I have other news, too."

Hearing Archer's amusement mixed with excitement, Lludd eased his hold and cocked his head.

His green eyes twinkling, Archer stated, "The mayor's bid to have me removed from office via a recall backfired." He chuckled, smirking. "Evidently, now *his* activities are being looked into by not just me, but some other organizations in the area." Laughing, Archer shook his head. "I think the mayor completely missed how many people were willing to come out after you guys took over the area. You've been a good influence on the town, and they don't like the idea of reverting, especially for a bigot."

Bodb barked a laugh. "We might have to find someone we like to run for mayor then." He smirked as his eyes turned vacant. "Hmm, I wonder who I can come up with."

Lludd didn't care about that. Not one bit. "This calls for

celebration," he cried before wrapping his arms around his sheriff. Knowing how much his mate loved being man-handled, Lludd lifted him and draped him over his shoulder. Then he started upstairs to the suite they used when at the ranch.

Hearing Archer's laugh coupled with the heady scent of his mate's arousal perfuming the air, Lludd knew his mate was on board with the idea.

So worth the wait. He's perfect for me.

You may also enjoy the following from eXtasy Books Inc:

Chumming with a Great Whale
Charlie Richards

Excerpt

Eban O'Gillie heard Ovram shout his name. Pushing to his feet, he rounded his desk and headed across the hall. He leaned against the open door and met the sea lion shifter's gaze.

"Yeah, Ov?" Eban asked, crossing his arms over his chest. "What's up?"

Ovram pointed at a security monitor. "I think we have an issue in the underwater aquarium."

Easing closer to the screen, Eban rested the knuckles of his left hand on the desk and took in the scene. The camera showed the wall of glass thirty feet away. Within the aquarium swam a vast array of fish, sharks, and other marine life.

Except, Eban knew that wouldn't be what Ovram was referring to. He swept his gaze over the large area full of milling humans who all appeared to be enraptured by the creatures beyond the glass. Well, all of them except one.

Near the far left side of the viewing room stood a man leaning against a wall. He clutched a cane in his right hand, and he stared at the floor. Even through the camera, Eban spotted the slight sheen of sweat dotting the man's brows as well as the pallor of his skin.

Even obviously under the weather, this guy is handsome.

Huh. Weird thought, but damn.

Eban couldn't help but sweep his gaze over the guy a second time. He figured he was a little over six feet, and his shoulders were wide with a trim waist. The jeans he wore molded to his muscular thighs. Eban even found the day or so growth of dark hair on his cheeks and chin sexy.

"Should I send someone in security to see if he needs assistance?"

Ovram's question yanked Eban out of his admiration of the man. He opened his mouth as he straightened, intending to nod and order him to contact Dare—an enforcer for their pod who worked under him in security. Except, then Eban felt the great white shark he shared his spirit with rumble in the back of his mind, displaying displeasure at sending the unmated giant octopus shifter to see to the man.

Ooookay.

Still, Eban would heed his animal's desires. "I'll go myself," he told their marine park's technological guru. "I was about to head to lunch anyway. Maybe he's diabetic and needs food."

With the other shifter's jaw sagging, Eban hustled out of the office, then the security building. He strode swiftly through the park, his long legs closing the distance between him and the hot man on the monitor. Eban really hoped he arrived before someone else had offered assistance.

Eban didn't understand his desire, but he wasn't one to second guess himself, and he never second guessed his shark's instincts.

Heading down the ramp that led into the tunnel that led to the underwater viewing areas, Eban easily dodged between viewers. He arrived in the room he wanted in just over five minutes. In that time, the man hadn't moved.

Eban spotted a woman glancing the guy's way, her brows creased in an expression of concern. Catching her eye, he smiled at her and tapped the word security on his World of Aquatica shirt. She smiled and nodded, then returned her attention to the children with her.

Pausing a couple of feet from the man, Eban inhaled, intending to speak. The man's fragrance coated his nostrils, and he almost let the breath out on a moan. The human's earthy, masculine aroma was just about the best damn thing Eban had ever scented.

Mate!

Eban sucked in a sharp gasp as the realization burst through his brain like a wrecking ball. Arousal surged through his body, causing his blood to flow south. His fingers twitched with the need to touch the man before him.

Then Eban took in the state of his mate once more.

Right. Gotta help him first.

Clearing his throat, Eban mentally pulled his head out of his ass. "Excuse me, sir," he greeted softly. When that didn't get the man to stop focusing on the floor, Eban stepped even closer and touched his elbow. "Sir?"

Wish I knew his name.

The human jolted from Eban's touch. His head snapped up even as his balance wobbled. A grunt of pain escaped his lips and he placed his free hand on the glass to steady himself.

"My apologies for startling you, handsome," Eban rumbled, gripping the man's upper arm in the hopes of offering support. "I'm Eban O'Gillie. I'm in security here. We thought you may need assistance."

The human's brown eyes narrowed a little as he looked up at him. "Why would I need assistance? I'm just standing here looking at the fish." As he spoke, he attempted to pull his arm from Eban's grip, but his unsteadiness made it difficult.

Even as Eban scented the lie he eased his grip and lifted both hands in placation. He immediately wanted to touch again. Still, since his mate didn't seem amenable to that, yet, he didn't.

"I don't mean to presume," Eban began slowly. Knowing the man really did need assistance, and with his shifter instincts screaming at him to care for his mate, he tried again. Eban didn't want to embarrass the man, so he pitched his voice low as he spoke. "You're pale. Your skin is clammy, and you seem a little unsteady on your feet." Giving the man an encouraging smile, Eban added, "If you're diabetic and need some food, I'd be happy to escort you to one of our restaurants."

"I—"

The human took a clearly painful step, snapping his mouth shut. Wincing and keeping quite a bit of weight on his cane and the other hand on the glass wall, he growled under his breath. He paused, heaved a sigh, then focused on Eban.

"Yeah, I guess I do need a hand. Overdid it," he grumbled. "I just need to get to the cart outside." Frowning, he muttered, "Getting down that ramp was harder than I thought it'd be."

Eban nodded. While he didn't understand what caused his mate's pain, it was obvious he was recovering from something. "I'd be happy to help." Slotting up close to the man, Eban wrapped his arm around his waist. His palm warmed where he rested it on the man's hip, feeling hard muscle beneath the jeans. "Lean on me, and we'll get you somewhere to get off what ails you."

"Thanks," the man mumbled, leaning against him and allowing him to help.

As they moved slowly up the ramp, Eban struggled with what to say. He'd never been the most sociable guy, but this was his mate. He needed to know at least something about him so he could find him again.

"I'm Eban," he repeated. "What's your name?"

"Graham," the human replied.

Eban nodded. "So, Graham, are you here with a group? Spouse? Family? Friends?" Realizing he sounded like he was putting the man through an inquisition, he quickly added,

"What brought you to World of Aquatica today?"

To Eban's relief, Graham answered his awkward questions.

"Came with Cuzco to see the tiger shark show." Graham hissed, pausing for a second. Beads of sweat popped out on his forehead. "He works here. You know him?"

"Yeah, I know Cuzco," Eban replied, nodding. The other shifter shared his spirit with a small coconut octopus. "I believe he just went on shift."

Which would explain why Graham was on his own.

Graham nodded. "Yeah."

They started moving again, and Eban saw the exit coming into view. His heartbeat sped up as he realized his time with his mate was coming to an end, and he still knew nothing about him.

"How do you know Cuzco?" Eban asked. At least he would have someone to ask about his mate after he left.

"He's my brother's partner. They're letting me crash in their spare bedroom for a while."

Upon hearing that, it was Eban's turn to pause.

That drew Graham's attention, and the man peered up at him. Something in Eban's expression must have concerned Graham, for he narrowed his eyes. "Don't tell me you're bigoted."

"What?" Get it together, idiot! "No. No, not at all." Eban winked at Graham. "You did here me call you handsome earlier, right?"

"Uhhh . . ."

Eban chuckled as he grinned down at him. Who he held in his arms finally clicking into place. His struggle with walking made sense now.

"You're Graham Canton, Grisham's brother." Upon seeing the wary nod, Eban squeezed Graham's hip and started them moving again. "Thank you for your service," Eban stated, holding his mate close as he referred to his time in the military.

And now he's home, here, and I'm gonna find a way to take care of him.

Except, even as Graham continued to move, his entire frame tensed in his arms. "How do you know about that?"

"I'm head of security," Eban revealed, trying to soothe him. At the same time, he smiled at Graham and gave a half-shrug. "I know just about everything that goes on around here."

ABOUT THE AUTHOR

Charlie started writing fantasy when she was eight, and after stumbling onto her first erotic romance at age nineteen, she realized her true calling. She now focuses on writing gay erotic romance, normally of the paranormal variety, with heroes of all kinds. With the help and support of her husband, Charlie finally fulfilled one of her life-long goals . . . move to acreage with her horses. You can often find her curled up with her laptop and a cup of tea or glass of wine, creating her next adventure. Charlie enjoys exploring the mountains of her new Oregon home on horseback, 4-wheeler, or motorcycle.

She can be reached at ch.richards2010@yahoo.com
Or visit her at www.charlie-richards.com

www.ingramcontent.com/pod-product-compliance
Lightning Source LLC
Chambersburg PA
CBHW060641130626
46555CB00002B/910